DESTROY THE CORRUPT

DESTROY THE CORRUPT

JUDGE, JURY, & EXECUTIONER BOOK TWO

CRAIG MARTELLE
MICHAEL ANDERLE

DISRUPTIVE IMAGINATION

LMBPN Publishing
PMB 196, 2540 South Maryland Pkwy
Las Vegas, NV 89109

First US edition, August 2018
Version 1.01, November 2018

Thanks to our Beta Readers

Micky Cocker
James Caplan
Kelly O'Donnell

Thanks to the JIT Readers

James Caplan
Kelly O'Donnell
Mary Morris
Keith Verret
Daniel Weigert
John Ashmore
Paul Westman
Peter Manis
Micky Cocker

If I've missed anyone, please let me know!

Editor
Lynne Stiegler

We can't write without those who support us
On the home front, we thank you for being there for us

We wouldn't be able to do this for a living if it weren't for our readers
We thank you for reading our books

A plasma beam hit the bulkhead above Rivka's head.

"Time to die, bitch!" a gruff voice yelled from beyond the overturned table. "I'm going to— Aaaggh!"

Rivka wanted to look, but the melting bulkhead still glowed. She didn't think her head would grow back if it was blasted off.

"All clear!" Vered called. "And next time, *before you deliver your verdict*, you might want to make sure the perp isn't armed."

Rivka peeked over the top of the table to confirm it was her bodyguard, nicknamed "Red," before standing. "Caught in the act *means* that they're probably armed. I couldn't let him get away, could I? Would you look at this?'

Rivka proudly displayed the scorch mark on her jacket, from the first shot that had narrowly missed and sent her diving for cover.

She pushed the table aside and stood over the dead body. "Justice is served, bitch."

"Amen to that, Magistrate." Red cleaned his blade on the dead man's shirt. "What's for lunch?"

"That new Mongolian place sounds promising..." Rivka tapped her datapad as she walked away. "Chaz, send the locals to clean this place up. Tell them that the case is closed and the paperwork will follow."

Red jumped over the growing blood puddle and caught up to the Magistrate. He moved smoothly past her and traveled in front, head on a swivel as he assessed high and low, left and right for threats. He was never off the clock.

"They were supposed to juice you enough to where you didn't overheat, not make you a man-mountain."

"That's my natural immensity," he replied.

"Is that a word?"

"If it isn't it should be, with my picture next to it in the dictionary." He talked as he walked, never looking at Rivka.

"Thanks for saving my ass."

"You should consider packing."

"Where are we going?" she asked.

"No. Packing heat, like a blaster or something. I'm pretty sure Grainger told you the same thing."

Rivka shook her head. "I don't think I will. You'll have to pack enough for both of us, and make sure you pack sandwiches, too. I'm hungry."

"You're always hungry, Magistrate."

"Alas, 'tis true, Vered." Rivka looked at the floor as she walked. It was how she thought best, even though Red gave her a hard time about not being more aware of her surroundings. Her mind was occupied. "And after lunch, I have a meeting with the other Magistrates. More boring lawyer training, and then we pick our next cases. I'll be quicker this time. Some kind of murder in paradise or a theft of shoes from a high-end shopping district. I could work cases like that. I hope they have snacks at the meeting, I'm hungry."

"I would like you to pay attention, please," Grainger said to the group. Jael and Cheese Blintz clinked their beer glasses before draining them and belching in unison. "The Federation's finest, ladies and gentlemen!"

Rivka scanned the area to see if anyone had heard. The restaurant side of the bar was empty, but even if people had been there, no one would have cared.

"Lighten up, Liebchen," Jael replied. "What case do you have for me, while I'm still sober enough to adjudicate it?"

"For you, we have the usual. File's in your folder. Go forth and conquer."

"Wait!" Rivka slapped her hand on the table, making the others jump. "Last time, it was all about being the first to raise your hand. Now, you're just handing them out? What bone job do I get this time?"

"'Bone job?' Sometimes the cases are a natural fit for our talents, so I assign them accordingly. Have you not read the *Magistrates' Manual*?"

"*Magistrates' Manual*?" Rivka looked at Chi, Jael, and lastly at Grainger. They nodded slowly. "You *suck*! When will the new-guy hazing end? As I learn the rules, you pack of Klingons circling Uranus change the rules. Here I am on the outside looking in, *again*. So, did I get a good case this time?"

"Your *last* case was a good case, Zombie! Damn. Maybe you want cookies for breakfast and ice cream for lunch? Don't answer that. You don't have a choice on this one. Nathan Lowell requested you to personally look into a competitor of the Bad Company."

"I get to see Terry Henry and Char again?" Rivka wondered, staring out the long window that showed space beyond the station.

"They're the Direct Action Branch. No, you'll be looking into the import/export business. Nathan believes that the Mandolin Partnership is a racket. Everywhere they've gone, people have been breaching their Bad Company contracts left and right. Businesses do that when they are afraid."

"Nathan picked me to bust up a racket?"

"They've already spread their influence to more than twenty worlds. They are based out of..." Grainger consulted his datapad, "the Corrhen Cluster."

"Never heard of it."

"No one has, but there's a Gate and they aren't afraid to use it."

"If no one's heard of them, how'd they grow so big so fast?"

"I can see why Nathan selected you for this case. Your insight is dazzling."

Rivka continued to look out the window, trying to remember the course she'd taken on racketeering and corruption. Finally, Grainger's words registered. She gave him the finger and then waved it back and forth. A server stood next to the table, silently watching.

When Rivka saw her, she stopped. "Sorry," she mumbled.

"One check?" the woman asked.

"Yes, and give it to *him*." Rivka pointed at Grainger. She finished the last of her fries. She wanted dessert, but since they had the check, she assumed the restaurant wanted the group to leave. "Can you get me the special lava cake disguised as a fudge brownie to go, please?"

The server updated the bill on her datapad and handed it to Grainger for confirmation. He tapped it, and the server left.

"I'll give odds you don't get your cake," Jael stated.

Rivka leaned her head sideways to look at her fellow Magistrate through one eye. "Them's angry words that can lead to no good," Rivka drawled. "I'm not leaving without my cake." Rivka changed gears. "Anyone up on the latest RICO laws?"

The other three Magistrates shook their heads. "Racketeer-Influenced and Corrupt Organizations," Grainger said. "I know what the acronym stands for, and that Bethany Anne brought it with her from Earth because of the massive corporations in the universe that turned whole planets into slaves, but I fear that's the extent of my knowledge. Looks like you get to spend some time in the library. We'll be in the gym."

"Wait!" Rivka called after the others got up to leave. "I haven't gotten my cake yet."

"You can owe me," Jael replied with a wink.

Red watched the others leave. He remained near the entrance, failing miserably at trying to look inconspicuous. The server appeared with a bag for Rivka. "I heard what they said." She smiled. "I brought you a double and charged your boss appropriately."

Rivka threw her head back and had a good laugh. "That's what I like to hear."

Red watched the interaction while glancing at the area outside the restaurant. He'd already assessed the waitstaff at the All Guns Blazing as a non-threat, but that didn't mean he would completely ignore them.

With a final nod at the kind server, Rivka strolled from the restaurant, lost in thought. Grainger was right—she needed to do some research before hitting the gym. She didn't have the choice to pick one over the other.

"No time to waste, Red!" she declared as she zoomed past. He hurried to get in front of her before stopping.

"Where are we going?"

"The Magistrates library." She tried to get past Red, but he held her back.

"Where is that?"

She pointed ahead, tucked her finger into her hand, and then pointed in the opposite direction. "Dammit, Grainger! There is no Magistrate's library, is there?" She took a deep breath. "Let's go to the briefing room. That will become the library."

Red nodded and headed in that direction. She saw Tyler Toofakre, the dentist as they rushed down the wide corridor of the restaurant and shop level of Federation Border Station 7. Rivka waved to him and called, "Tomorrow, seven in the morning for breakfast?"

"Sure," the man replied as he strolled casually toward the elevator. He gave her a thumbs-up before disappearing behind a crowd.

"What is that about?" Red asked, no judgment in his voice. He wanted to know for security reasons.

"I realized I need normal in my life. If I spend too much time with the likes of Jael, Grainger, and Cheese Blintz, I will be a basket case in short order. He is the most normal person I've met out here. We have to stay grounded in some way."

"While in space?"

"Exactly."

"Did you get the server's name?"

"What?" Rivka was confused. "Do you have to run a background check or something?"

"Eventually. Maybe tomorrow you can get her number for me." Red continued to scan the area.

"Are we in high school?" Rivka chuckled at Red's scowl. "Fine. I'll ask her tomorrow if she needs a man-mountain in her life."

"Tell her I'm a nice guy."

"By all the stars in the universe, I shall condemn you for eternity if you strike up a relationship with her, it goes bad, and I don't get to eat there anymore!"

"I share your concern," Red replied, tinging his statement with the right amount of sarcasm. "Us servant types need to stick together."

"Is that how you think I treat you?" Rivka was instantly upset. She grabbed Red's massive arm and spun him around. Her golden-blue hazel eyes flashed as she glared at him.

His look wasn't confrontational. "I seek no one above my station," Red said calmly. "I think I have more in common with someone like her than someone like you, and no, I'm not hitting on you. That's not my thing. She observes people and works them to earn their praise and maybe a tip. I observe people and try to understand what they are capable of. We both share a sense of duty. She wears the All Guns Blazing logo with pride. I wear my service to the Magistrates with pride, too. We aren't so different. Just tell her I'm a nice guy."

"I'll tell her you don't bite."

"What if that's not true?" Red's gaze flashed past Rivka for a moment before returning to her.

"What are you trying to do to me?"

"In a battle for your life, there is no such thing as a fair fight. I'll bite someone's nose off if I have to. I'm not going to lose a fight. Ever."

"Here's what I'll tell her: 'I'll give you fifty credits if you'll talk to my bodyguard.' Will that work?"

"I am doomed to be forever alone." Red took the stairs as he preferred to do. They traveled in silence since others were in the stairwell, then followed two smaller corridors to reach the briefing room. Once Rivka confirmed it was empty, she checked the time and turned back to Red.

"Give me four hours. I'll lock myself in, so you can consider yourself off-duty. Why don't you go back there and talk to her yourself? You *are* a nice guy, Red, easy on the eyes and loyal to what you believe in. Give her a chance to like you, and you'll be saving me fifty credits."

Rivka closed and secured the door before Red could respond. She set her datapad to the side and opened the bag, delighting in the chocolatey goodness wafting into the air. "Come to me, my friend," Rivka told the double serving of lava cake.

R ivka rolled her head back and forth to ease the stiffness in her neck. She used the room's systems to project passages of law on the big screen while researching case precedents on her datapad.

"Lexi, bundle those last ten cases and display every reference for predicate offenses."

"Of course, Magistrate. I love researching the law. As an Artificial Intelligence, I am constantly gaining new insight into the human psyche. Each Magistrate researches and studies differently. Jael dispenses with case law in entirety and delivers her own interpretation of the law as promulgated by the Federation. She says that she is a judge, and her determinations will provide precedent for those who follow. Chi puts his weight behind precedent, but he looks for the penalties first, giving weight to those with the harshest punishments."

"I would have guessed differently—that Jael would be all about the punishment and Chi would prefer setting precedent. What about Grainger?"

"Grainger has never studied the law with me."

"That is interesting. Is he just making it up? Maybe it's as simple as, 'He works out, and he knows things.'"

"I cannot say," the AI replied.

"Fair enough." Rivka scrolled through the predicate offenses. "There have to be at least two of the predicate offenses such as murder, kidnap, arson, drug dealing, and so on. Those are all felonies, and they must attach to an enterprise, not an individual. Enterprise and predicate are critical factors in charging under RICO instead of charging just the crimes. Racketeering is the umbrella under which the rest of this garbage happens. How is that different from conspiracy?"

"Conspiracy is when two or more people agree to commit a crime and intend to see it through. There is an intent component as well as an act, but the act is challenging to prove before a crime is committed. It is usually applied *post facto* as an additional charge and sentencing factor for the main crime."

"Got it. Just like RICO, there are both civil and criminal versions. I'm not their mom to tell them to play nice with their contracts, so forever more, unless I specifically ask, don't show me the civil side of the law. I mete out Justice to criminals." Rivka slapped her hand on the table for emphasis.

"Is that what the Pretarian Treaty was?"

"If you have any sway at all with Grainger, no more tall-alien civil disputes or war-starting disagreements. Give me crimes so I can find and punish criminals. Give the offended-people disputes to Grainger."

"I don't have anything to do with the case selection. I am sorry, Rivka. You seem passionate about this point."

"I love the law," Rivka said as she rested her chin on the table. "I'm tired of looking through this stuff, which means my four hours are up. I'm going to the gym."

"You've been here forty-seven minutes."

Rivka's mouth fell open. "You must be mistaken. It has to be at least three hours. I'm hungry again."

"I am good at many things, and keeping the time is one of them. Forty-seven minutes, Magistrate."

Rivka perked up. "That means the others will still be at the gym. A little sparring with my brothers, maybe kick Jael upside her no-cake-for-you face. How does that sound?"

"Vindictive and mean."

Rivka turned off the screen and powered down her datapad. "It's all in the spirit of getting better at what we do, Lexi. I'm sure they want to kick my ass, too. Don't let Red know that I've gone on without him. I'll make it back before he returns. Where is he, by the way?"

"At All Guns Blazing. He is at a table by himself."

"*Shit.*" Rivka wanted to leave him to his own devices, but couldn't because her conscience would punish her for abandoning him. Rivka set out for the stairs to the restaurant level.

Rivka flopped down in the seat opposite Red and he jerked in surprise. "What are you doing here?"

11

"The better question is why are you sitting alone?" Rivka asked.

"Because Lindy doesn't get off for another hour and then we're going to take a walk. Damn! I'm back on the clock. Let me tell her that I have to cancel." Red rose and started looking around.

"Sit down!" Rivka ordered. "You didn't see me walk in, and now you have to look for her instead of just knowing where she is? You are far too distracted to work efficiently, so you have to take the rest of the day off. I will see you in the morning. I promise not to get killed between now and then."

Red scanned the area before reaching into his coat. He shielded something with his hand as he pushed it toward the Magistrate. "Take it."

She looked at the small pistol and wondered how Red could pull the trigger. "Let me guess, your backup to the backup?"

Red held up five fingers. *The fifth backup.*

"Lindy, huh?" Rivka slid the pistol into her lap, tested its feel, and slipped it into the inside pocket of her jacket. "Good luck, big man. Don't do anything I wouldn't do," she told him as she walked briskly away. As soon as she left the restaurant, she almost bumped into a man and a woman. The woman dropped her purse and it burst open, and Rivka stopped to help her collect her things. The man and the woman leaned in together, scooping things back into the purse.

The man apologized as he bumped into Rivka when he stood. The Magistrate knew something was wrong. She grabbed the woman's arm, instantly sensing the scam. She elbowed the woman in the head and turned to give her full attention to the man, only to find the pistol Red has given her to carry aimed at her face. Rivka's eyes focused on the end of the barrel. It was shaking slightly, but not enough for her to act.

A massive arm looped under the pistol, knocking it upward as the hand slammed into the criminal's throat. Rivka caught the pistol as it fell from numb fingers. She put it back into her coat before turning her attention to the woman, still moaning from a broken face. The man's face turned purple and his eyes rolled back in his head before Red let go, dropping the perp to the deck.

Rivka pulled her datapad out. "Lexi, please dispatch station security to All Guns Blazing to pick up two perps guilty of theft. The threat-to-Magistrate charge will be delayed until I think about it a little bit. They are to be held in separate cells until I deliver a final judgment. Oh, and they'll need medical attention, too."

"I take my eyes off you for ten seconds..."

"Do you think he would have fired?" Rivka asked, not so sure the man had it in him to commit murder.

"He *could* have, which is all that matters to me."

Lindy stood at the entrance to All Guns Blazing. Red smiled and waved.

"I'll take care of things here," Rivka told him before she saw the look on the server's face. "On second thought, you wait here."

Rivka hurried to Lindy before she could run away. "I'm Magistrate Rivka Anoa. Red is my bodyguard, and he's the best I've ever seen."

"I'm Lindy," the woman replied. "I don't know what I just saw. So violent."

"What you saw was the commission of a crime by well-practiced criminals. They are predators, and have no place where decent people live. They have been judged and found wanting."

"Is that what you do?" Lindy watched Red as he tried not to look back.

"That is what I do. Red makes sure that I can do it without interference. He just saved my life, and I don't take that lightly. I feel safe when he's around. Maybe that's why I got into that situation—because he makes it easy for me to be trusting. If you'll excuse me, I need to go. I hope we get to see you again."

"I look forward to it," Lindy replied.

Rivka panted heavily. She was covered in sweat and bruises that were already healing.

"You are much better than you used to be!" Grainger said, trying not to sound demeaning.

"She must have been really bad before if this is what you call progress," Jael muttered. She was also covered in sweat and bruises.

"I'm too tired to even flip you the bird."

"I know what you mean. I'm also jagging you. You fight well, but this guy lives for this shit." Jael pointed with her chin.

Chi lay in the middle of the mat performing a perfect dead-man pose. Grainger flexed and shadow-boxed.

"On that note," Rivka started, "what law school did you go to?"

Grainger stopped punching and stepped over Chi on his way to take a seat on the bench beside Rivka. "Hard Knocks U?"

"You're not a lawyer, are you?"

"No, and neither are you. I'm a Magistrate, and we mete out justice."

"But only in accordance with the law," Rivka countered.

"Of course."

"So where did you learn the law?"

"Are you judging *me*, Magistrate?" Grainger asked with a cold edge. "I didn't go to law school, but I studied hard because I had to if I was going to help the other..." he looked around to make sure no one was listening, "Rangers make the transition. There were more Rangers than anyone ever knew. We embraced our new mission, and we couldn't do that openly by going through the gateway of academic approval. I'll tell you that our taskmaster was as rigorous as your school."

"I went to law school on the *Meredith Reynolds*, thank you very much."

"'The Queen's Barrister' before you were a lawyer. I know. Tell me a story, Magistrate Rivka."

"I was a nobody who did well in school, saw some shit I didn't like, and figured that people needed lawyers, as ridiculous as that sounds. Finished undergrad in three years, and immediately started the Reynolds Legal Academy. In my final year, Bethany Anne herself made an appearance. She spent a fair amount of time on the QBBS *Meredith Reynolds*, but I'd never seen her before. I often saw that hunk of man candy known as John Grimes, but I digress. He was a Ranger, wasn't he?"

"Common misconception. No, he was never a Ranger, but that's because he was the Head Bitch. Something completely different. He could have been a Ranger, but that wasn't what Bethany Anne needed from him," Grainger explained.

"BA stopped by the table where I was in the middle of a test. She wanted to talk. Who was I to deny the Queen? But the clock was ticking. It put me in a quandary. BA found it funny. She took my test pad off my desk and broke it in half. I was crushed. Instant failure. All I saw was three years of hard work down the drain, quick as that. BA's smile was infectious. I knew it would be okay, but I still wanted to prove myself by acing the test.

"The Queen put her hand on my shoulder and looked into my eyes so deeply I think she saw all the way to my soul.

"She let go and said, 'You are special. You see things, don't you?' I've always had the ability to see random emotions but never thought much of it. I thought of it as intuition, nothing more. I stumbled through an incoherent answer, but BA stopped me. 'I am making you the Queen's Barrister. It is what you will be from this moment forward. Even though you haven't graduated yet, you will. Don't fuck it up. I'll call in my marker at some point. You'll know it when you see it. Make me proud, Rivka Anoa—proud that we have fucking laws and people like you out there helping the universe's twatwaffles understand what it takes to comply with them.' And then she walked away."

"That's it?" Grainger asked, disappointment painted

across his face. "I was expecting something more epic than she made me fail a test, I felt bad, and she gave me a title to make me feel better."

"Is that what you heard?"

Jael and Grainger both nodded. Chi twitched enough to show that he wasn't dead.

"You have to be the worst listener of all time," Rivka told Grainger before continuing, "No epic space battles. It was school, a sedate environment, where we fought the good fight within an established framework. Turns out that I was pretty good at it, as you know."

"I wouldn't know a good lawyer if one washed up dead on the beach."

"And now you are one!" Rivka said as she poked Grainger in the chest. "I need to scrub off the stench of kicking your ass."

"You called me a good lawyer! Thank you. I am all that and more. You can scrub and scrub, and it won't change the sweet smell of my victory." Grainger helped Chi up. "When are you guys heading out?"

"Tomorrow," Jael replied. "It's a short hop and a boring case. I'm in no hurry."

Chi's eyes rolled around in his head. His mouth worked, but no words came out.

"Tomorrow for me as well. I need to rescue Jay from her spa weekend," Rivka replied.

"Are you going to see about getting her some Pod-doc time?" Grainger wondered.

"Not yet. I don't know if she'll stay on the team. I'm not pushing her one way or another. She seems to like it, though."

"If she stays, think about it. She's painting a mural in your rec room, and I'd like to see what the finished product looks like," Grainger said while picking at his fingernails.

"It's coming out quite nicely. It's the story of her life, it seems, painted on the backdrop of space. It's peaceful and violent, beautiful and ugly, but always hopeful."

"You should be a politician with that waffly bullshit."

"Isn't that what lawyers do when they've had enough of lawyering?" Rivka went in to the locker room, turned on the shower, and let it rain over her. She could feel the power that the nanocytes were restoring to her body. They worked on the inside, and she scrubbed the outside while her mind churned through RICO.

3

"A little more of that, please," Jay requested in a silken voice. The alien masseuse used all four of his hands to work the young woman's back. Oil glistened in the soft lights.

"If you'll please excuse me," a female voice inserted.

The masseuse stopped. Jay sighed and pulled her face from the padded hole in the table. "Yes?"

"You have an urgent call. It sounds official, and they wouldn't take no for an answer."

"Was it a woman? Called herself Magistrate?" Jay wondered waving for the woman to hand over the comm device.

"Yes?" Jay said again.

"Jay! So glad to hear your voice. You must have missed my earlier message about the team meeting tonight. We're heading out first thing in the morning. Are you coming with us?"

"I've been here all day and didn't get any messages, so I must compliment the staff on their duty to their guests."

Jay nodded to the woman, who smiled in reply. "Going with you is my job, isn't it?"

"As long as you want it. You've proven yourself, so you're on the team. We need to talk about this next case. It could be dangerous."

"I expect that's how all your cases will be. They wouldn't send the Queen's Barrister if it were a milk run."

"I'm the newest Magistrate, so these *are* the milk runs. Maybe they're the shit details. I have yet to figure out which. All Guns Blazing in thirty minutes."

"Do you ever eat anywhere else?"

"I like their food."

"Of course you do. Quantity over quality."

"That strikes a dagger into my heart. I am reeling from the verbal blow as if pierced by a Bungholian war spear. I'd like to think we get high quality at a good price. Plus, AGB Enterprises is a wholly owned Team BMW asset, a friend to the Bad Company who does favors for the Federation all the time. It's best to stay on their good side."

"Fine. See you there." Jay gave the comm device back and pulled the towel over her as she sat up. "That's it. My spa retreat is over."

"I am so sorry to hear that, Miss Jay. You have been our special and favored guest these past three days. You are an exquisite example of the finest culture."

"If my parents heard that, they wouldn't believe it." Jay smiled at the woman and nodded at the alien, who quietly excused himself to allow Jay to get dressed in private. "I don't know when I'll be back, but I guarantee I'm going to need another three days in the spa."

"You're bringing a date to our mission briefing?" Rivka asked, looking down her nose at the big man.

"You make it sound like a bad thing. You know what they say about too much work," Red replied casually. "Besides, I ran a background check. She's clean."

Rivka punched him in the shoulder. "Fine. Tell her it's confidential."

Jay sauntered into the restaurant wearing a new dress and new shoes and carrying a handbag. Red raised an eyebrow. "What happened to our juvenile delinquent?"

Rivka smiled and clapped softly. "I like the new you. You look gorgeous!"

"Thank you," she told Rivka before looking sternly at Red. "Not you, barbarian."

She started to take the seat next to Red, but Rivka stopped her. "You're over here. Red has a date." Rivka pointed to the seat next to her.

Jay looked confused. "What's a date?" she asked, feigning innocence and batting her eyes.

"It's what you and I don't get, but he does."

"You have a date tomorrow!" Red blurted.

"Breakfast with the dentist? That's not a date. It's different than this."

"How?" Red asked slowly.

"When I come up with a witty and sharp reply to that, I'll let you know."

Lindy strolled down the passageway, dressed casually in jeans and a button-down. She stopped to talk with the host at the front. Red waved, and Rivka snickered behind her hand. "How in the world would she miss you?"

Red gestured her to silence, then stood and pulled Lindy's chair out for her. "Lindy, Jay. Jay, Lindy," Red completed the introductions.

"I hope we don't bore you to tears," Rivka began. "We need to talk about my next case. We sometimes refer to them as 'missions,' and ourselves as 'the team.' I may be the Magistrate, but I can't do what I do all by myself."

"I understand," Lindy said. "Red tells me that this is confidential. I'm good at keeping secrets, I'd like to think. You should hear some of the things customers tell me, but then again, if they're telling a perfect stranger is it *really* a secret?"

"I like the way you think," Rivka stated with a definitive nod. "As soon as we order, we'll get down to business."

"I don't want to be too forward, but I've ordered for us, and it is already being taken care of. You won't find it anywhere on the menu. Red wanted something special for each of you," Lindy explained.

The corners of Rivka's mouth twitched upward.

"I guarantee you won't be disappointed," Red added.

"As long as it isn't Turbid Pie, I'm sure we'll be fine," Jay said.

"Turbid Pie?" Lindy wondered.

"The most disgusting stuff in the galaxy. It's toxic to humans, but the Keome and Pretarians consider it a delicacy. It completely stunk up our ship."

"You have your own ship?"

Rivka nodded. "A corvette. It's small, but it has some special upgrades just for us."

"What's her name?"

Red pointed to Rivka, who pointed to Jay, who pointed back at Red.

"We haven't picked a name, yet," Red answered.

"How can you not have a name for your ship?" Lindy pressed.

"I said that I can't have my baby without a name, but here we are, nameless and unloved. Corvette Seven Seven Four suffices until the right name comes along. In the meantime, we have an Entity Intelligence called Chaz on board to fly the ship. We are only passengers. Chaz is the bomb."

"Don't forget Hamlet." Jay showed the cat's size with her hands. "A cat that lives on the ship."

"You have a cat?"

"He's worth his weight in gold. I don't think I'll ever forget how Yus came out of his shoes when Hamlet jumped on him." Jay started to laugh.

The food arrived, seafood salads for Jay and Lindy, a massive bistok steak for Red, and a platter of hamburgers and fries for Rivka.

"Very funny, Red, but I accept your tribute. You get a reprieve, but tomorrow I'll most likely find you guilty of something and condemn you to spend the rest of your life on Jhiordaan. And before you ask, no, you can't take a date."

Rivka winked at Red.

"Better dig in before it gets cold," Red said, grabbing his fork while making his own knife appear from somewhere, leaving the restaurant's blade untouched.

Rivka offered a toast, forcing Red to stop, his first

square of steak halfway to his mouth. He put it down, still speared by the fork, and raised his glass. "To friends and the rule of law."

"Weren't you in here last night?" the hostess asked.

"I eat every meal in here," Rivka admitted.

"You should get a Frequent Patron card."

"I should buy stock. I see who I'm meeting." Rivka waved and headed inside.

Tyler sat at the table engrossed in his pad. He looked up when Rivka pulled her chair out. "Whatcha reading?"

"A new Kurtherian Gambit book, released this morning. I think it's number nine thousand or something. I've read them all."

"How do you read nine thousand of anything?"

"I have a subscription and lots of time."

"Dentisting isn't what you thought it would be?"

"It's great—better than I thought—but with modern advances, people rarely have dental issues. When they do, that's where I come in. I have to stay up on the latest procedures, but usually those entail punching buttons on the equipment. And how about your gig? Magistrating living up to what you thought it would be?"

"That and more. Never a dull moment. As soon as we're finished eating, I have to head back into space."

"I guess we better order, then. I don't want to hold up the long arm of the law." Tyler waved to get the server's attention. "Why don't they have electronic ordering like all the other places?"

"Old-school. They like the personal touch. I come here a lot."

The server took their order and left.

"I'll be looking into alleged racketeering. I might have to visit some twenty-one planets on this trip."

"Wow! I've only been to three different planets in my life. I need to get out more, but I can't let the practice fall into disrepair. I have a reputation to uphold."

"Always there when needed?" Rivka ventured.

"I should probably change it to that, but no. It's Dentistry Done Right." Tyler looked to make sure no one was listening before leaning close and whispering conspiratorially, "I tell everyone that the other guy's slogan is No Pain, No Gain."

"That's Doctor Payne, right? No Payne, No Gain. I kind of like it."

"But you're not supposed to like pain," Tyler countered.

"I don't." Rivka shook her head. "I bring the pain."

"I don't understand."

"Mete out justice. Sometimes punishment is warranted, and that's our charter. Magistrates can deliver the punishment on the spot."

"Do you mean, kill people? Have *you* killed people?"

Rivka was taken aback. She didn't want to be flippant about killing people who deserved to die, or that she had a special ability. "Would it matter if I had?"

"You have! But I don't want to hear about it. I have a certain view of you that I want to hold onto," Tyler declared, a range of emotions crossed his face before he restored his normal exterior. "Le femme fatale with roles reversed."

"You said you read a lot. I understand."

"A lot. How is your cat?"

"Hamlet is a trooper. The ship is kind of small, but he keeps himself entertained. Chaz takes care of him. It's strange, to say the least."

"You know cats are nature's purest killers, but they're only five kilos in size. That leaves them perpetually angry at the universe in a cute and cuddly package."

"I doubt Hamlet has ever killed anything. He lives on a sterile starship."

"No sun to shine in the window, no birds to watch, no vermin to kill. Poor Hamlet."

"Outside of abhorring physical contact with humans, he seems fine. Maybe he's an alien?"

"Maybe they're all aliens."

4

"Red? A word, please." Rivka crooked a finger for her bodyguard to follow. Once on the bridge, she secured the hatch and turned on him. "You can't bring your squeeze on a mission."

"She's not my squeeze!"

Rivka rested her chin on her chest. "That's not the point."

"Then why say it? Aren't words your best tool?" Red argued.

Rivka closed her eyes and took a deep breath before continuing, "Why is she here?"

"She took vacation, and you know the three of us can't handle everything you need to do."

"But you should have checked with me first." Rivka put her hands on her hips and tried to glare, but knew that she was glad of the company. "We can't take on any more strays."

Red wore a reserved smile. "I think she's the only one who's *not* a stray. Maybe she won't fit in after all."

"Maybe not. We'll be back here soon enough, although this could be a long one. Did you see that list of planets? That's a Big Bertha buttload. I think we may have to go to them all, collect information, consolidate, and analyze. We're on a scavenger hunt, Red. This is going to be an awful lot of mind-numbing digging through data."

"Good thing you have an expert in that area whose mind never goes numb," Chaz interjected.

"You're going to be a busy guy on this one, Chaz. Thanks for stepping up."

"My pleasure, Magistrate. Where are we going?"

"We're going to start with two planets based on gambling, S'Korr and Show Low. They seem the most vulnerable for external interference in their affairs. Not that that is illegal, but that's what we're looking for. They are called 'predicate crimes.' Without them, there is no racketeering. Without enterprise involvement, there is no racketeering. This could be a difficult case to adjudicate. I will need everyone's help, including Lindy's."

Rivka gave Red a thumbs-up before they returned to the mess deck. "Welcome aboard, Lindy. Consider yourself a member of the team. You'll have a role to play, although I can't tell you what it will be yet. We change depending on the circumstances. In nearly all cases, Red will be with me. Protecting me is his primary job. I need you to be good with that—except when I'm carrying his big ass because he's passed out."

"He didn't tell me about that." Lindy looked up at Red.

"It never came up, and for what it's worth, she's much stronger than she looks. Let me show you your room."

"My own room? I thought they shared bunks on

spaceships," Lindy replied coquettishly as Red quickly ushered her away. Rivka watched them go. From the bridge, Chaz started playing the theme song to *The Love Boat*.

Jay, now sporting rainbow-colored hair, continued to paint, adding color to sections of her mural she'd previously finished. Rivka looked closely at it. Some of the painting had been dark, but it was growing lighter as Jay touched it up.

"Our past becomes less horrific when the future is bright," Rivka stated.

"The darkness of our past lightens over time," Jay replied, "when the sun shines on its shadows. We are what we make of ourselves."

"When we control that which is within our control, yes. Those who count on luck will never see the light of day. A cloud will forever hang over their heads."

"We must read the same things. Next time, you'll have to come with me to the spa. It was a magnificent three days."

"You spent three whole days at the spa?" Rivka asked.

"Yes, the Royal Executive Package."

"Am I paying you that much?" Rivka pursed her lips and stared at the wall. She had no idea what anyone was getting paid, including herself. Grainger handled that and never bothered telling anyone what they were good for besides food and lodging.

"Don't forget who my parents are."

"But they think you're in jail."

"I still have access to the credit chip, and it has a very large line of credit." Jay grinned.

"Once they figure out you're not in jail, they'll send someone after you, and then we'll both be in trouble."

"You give them too much credit. They will be happy to know that I'm okay without actually having to do anything. Trust me on this."

"I'm not sure if I should feel sorry or happy for you, but as you wish. We'll leave it be. I'll come up with something if a collector shows up at our door looking for you."

"That's why I like the idea of living on a spaceship."

Rivka grunted approval and returned to the bridge. "We have work to do, Chaz. Pull up the information on S'Korr, please."

S'Korr, a sports arena-type planetary economy with overpriced beverages and snacks, plus cheap team logo knickknacks and a massive sports book operation. On S'Korr, a patron could bet on any sport within the galaxy. The planetary data appeared first—climate, size, population centers—and then Chaz presented the governmental structure. It looked like a star chart, not a typical hierarchy with someone at the top. She held her head in her hands as she tried to make sense of it. "What are you showing me, Chaz? That is one fucked-up system."

"It works for them. You will need to meet with no fewer than seven different entities, none of whom are required to work with the others. They stay in their lanes, so to speak."

"Those lanes have to converge somewhere."

"They do not, at least from a leadership perspective."

"Start arranging meetings for me, Chaz. If there is a most important person, get that one first. After that, best you can manage in order of priority. I'm going to work out.

I sense some frustration coming on and don't want to take it out on the poor gamblers from S'Korr."

Chaz retracted the furniture that cleared the space on the mess deck. She started with the magnetically-activated weight bar and pounded out a set.

Red appeared in his workout clothes, as did Lindy. Jay was miffed at having to stop painting. "Join us," Rivka offered.

"Have we left the station already?" she asked.

"I don't think so," Rivka answered with a shrug. "We're buttoned up and ready to go. You know Chaz will have us there in no time, and then we might get distracted. Can't miss the workouts. Our lives may depend on being in shape—like how you beat the bomb on Pretaria. Our physical prowess is our safety net."

Rivka was talking to Lindy as much as Jay. Red never missed a workout, and often added exercises to focus on a particular muscle group or special ability. "We need a firing range in here," Red mumbled.

"We have one—virtually of course—that I have linked to replicas of your standard Federation weaponry."

"If only I *used* standard Federation weaponry." Red smirked and nodded. "That will do, Chaz. As soon as we're done, we'll send some rounds downrange. Lindy needs to get accustomed to the firepower we may employ. Just in case."

"I have no intention of *shooting* anyone!" she exclaimed crossing her arms on her chest.

"That's good," Rivka agreed. "We have no intention of shooting anyone, either, but sometimes it just happens. The better you are with weapons, the better you can use them to bluff. Imagine if you were able to shoot a weapon out of someone's hand? You don't get hurt, and they don't get hurt, or not much anyway."

"I'll have to think about it."

Jay held up her hands. "Not even going to pick up a weapon."

"You are the young and innocent member of the group. We have to keep someone outside the fray. We don't need you shooting a weapon," Rivka said.

"Who says *I'm* not young and innocent?" Lindy asked.

"We can't have everyone on board unwilling to fire a weapon." Rivka scowled.

"Fine. I'll do it, but I prefer not to. I don't want to put that burden on our seventeen-year-old."

"I've been around the block!" Jay tried to stand tall, but it only made her look scrawny.

"Everyone learns how to fire a weapon, and everyone learns how to fight. That's the new team rule. We never know what kind of crap we're going to get ourselves into. Just because you know how doesn't mean you have to do it without thinking. We don't shoot people in the back. We don't fire without aiming. We don't fire at all when we don't have to."

"This will be fun," Red mumbled as he stretched and pulled the punching bag down to hit it bare-handed a few times. Lindy got on the other side, braced herself, and nodded. Red leaned into his punches, hitting the bag harder and harder.

"Keep your hand up," Rivka suggested. "Someone's going to pop you in the face while you're swinging those haymakers."

Red raised his hands to make sure that one always blocked his face. The skin on his knuckles was torn but healed rapidly. His new nanocytes were engaged. "Thanks for the upgrade, Magistrate."

"Do all members of the team get the nanocytes?" Lindy asked.

Rivka dialed the bar heavier and pounded out another set in lieu of answering.

"The powers that be prefer not, because once you're upgraded, you carry the nanos for life. A much *longer* life. They had to make sure I was in this for the full ride. Imagine if I was evil, what I could do being able to heal this quickly and survive extreme heat?"

"You'd still prefer air conditioning," Rivka sniped. "I know I do. That place was like Hell's own furnace. Fuck that."

"Jay is a hardened criminal, so she's on probation." Red winked at the young woman, and she saluted with a paint-brush. "I think you're the only one here who isn't cast off from society."

"How is the Magistrate a castoff?" Lindy asked, taking one of Red's hands and rubbing it where the knuckles had healed as she looked at Rivka.

"We will leave that for another day. Let's spar. Some defensive moves for Lindy and Jay while I kick your ass. I'm still miffed at having to carry you."

"I'm still miffed that you had to carry me, but thankful you did. Don't take it personally when I punch you in the face. Repeatedly."

"That will be the day," Rivka taunted, wondering how

much faster Red had gotten after his Pod-doc treatment. *Better keep your hands up*, she told herself.

The corvette burst into space outside S'Korr's lunar orbit. A smaller planet, S'Korr circled a k-class star. With a minimal population, but a massive tourist trade and a Gate with an active digital pipeline, all the galaxy's games were streamed in real-time. The technology to make that happen had been developed for other purposes, but the founders of S'Korr saw opportunity, as budding entrepreneurs do. They seized it, and S'Korr became one of the top three betting havens. The Gate was filled with scheduled traffic, but that had no bearing on the Magistrate's ship.

With its own Gate, the corvette could skip the lines, but it couldn't get past the parade of ships heading to or returning from the planet's surface.

"Insanity!" Rivka declared. "How long to get to the planet, Chaz?"

"Several hours. Not because we can't bypass the traffic, but there is no place to park at the spacedrome. We need to park at the spacedrome to get ground transportation for you to travel to your meetings. I've secured a limousine service. Your first appointment is in four hours with a Mister K'Leptus, head of Best Sports Book."

"Lindy?" Rivka called. The woman appeared. With brown hair and brown eyes, she stood in stark contrast to the crew's other women. Red had shaved his head, making him look the starkest of all. "Have you ever gambled before?"

"Probably too much," she said.

She shook her head. "Would you know a fixed match if you saw one?"

"Between the two of us we might," Jay offered.

"What do you think, Red?"

"I think two good-looking women in a sports book will be treated like hookers no matter how they're dressed."

"That wasn't my question, but I don't think you're wrong. Can we use that to our benefit, or do they play up their naïveté and find someone who is smart to give them a hand in spending their credits?"

"That's not really my thing," Jay said, looking at the floor.

"I'll teach you what you need to know, but if anyone touches me, I'm breaking their arm, tentacle, or whatever protuberance gets shoved my way."

Red nodded approvingly. "We have time. Let me teach you a few moves." The women returned to the mess deck since it was currently configured for working out, and Red started his instruction. Rivka remained on the bridge.

"One more time, Chaz. Federation statutes regarding theft and gambling..."

5

Red was the first off the ship. He was traveling heavy, carrying the shotgun and wearing his ballistic vest and leggings. S'Korr had no military, but each booking joint had its own small army of security. They'd been informed about Red. Time would tell if they listened.

Lindy and Jay came off the ship well after the Magistrate and Red had caught a limousine to the Best Sports Book. They were dressed casually, and after a short walk through the arrivals terminal, grabbed a taxi to the Best Sports Book.

That was the plan, and also a check to evaluate the quality of the planet's intelligence apparatus. Red suspected that Lindy and Jay would be associated with the Magistrate and treated differently, even though he had floated the idea that the patrons would think of the women as hookers. Rivka didn't think the two women would be linked to her. The bet was the next dinner out, paid for from personal funds.

Which reminded Rivka to check her account.

"First time on S'Korr?" the limo driver asked.

Red activated the privacy panel, and the driver disappeared behind an electronic screen.

"What did you do that for?"

"That guy doesn't need to know jack shit about you, Magistrate."

"That guy may be our key to getting treated like decent human beings in this place. You never know which person is the one you need to impress. Now open the screen." Red hesitated. "I'm not fucking around, Red."

The screen disappeared.

"Yup, first time. Any recommendations?"

"Bet the mins at BSB, then go to Better Sports Betting, or as we like to call it, BSB Lite. You'll do better there. I could take you there right now if you'd like."

"No. I won't be gambling."

"Then what are you here for, and with a bodyguard to boot?"

"Meet with some of the key business owners and leaders of S'Korr. The Federation needs information, and I'm here to get it."

"What are you, some kind of accountant?"

"Lawyer," Rivka said proudly.

"Shit, lady, they're going to have fun with you!"

Red turned to reach through the opening, but Rivka grabbed his arm. "Wait until he stops. I don't want to be in an accident. On second thought, just let him go." She pointed to the privacy button. The electronic screen materialized, muting the driver's peals of laughter.

Rivka chuckled. "I guess Chaz left out some important

details." She accessed her pad. "Chaz, is this a male-dominated society, and what do they have against lawyers?"

"Yes, it is male-dominated, and the legal profession is outlawed. The people who handle the contract work for S'Korr are called 'contractors.'"

"Next time, Chaz, don't leave that part out."

Red smiled. "Men are in charge, and lawyers are illegal. I like this place."

"What am I going to do with you, Red?" Rivka shook her head slowly as she smirked at her bodyguard.

"I recommend you don't tell anyone you're a lawyer."

"And we would not have had that tidbit of knowledge had we not engaged with the driver. Thank the Queen that *women* are in charge!"

Red smiled. "Thank the Queen indeed that I get a job like this. Thanks, boss, for carrying me out of Pretaria and saving my life. Who else would do that for their bodyguard? We are expendable, if you haven't figured that out."

"You're not expendable, for the simple reason that I don't have time to train a new one. At least you're housebroken. Mostly."

"Save the bullshit for someone who doesn't know you. Loyalty goes both ways. You're the only boss I've ever had who understood that. So, can I punch Happy Driver in his face when we stop, or maybe I'll jack him upside his ghoulies?"

"Just tell him to wait for us. I know he'll run the meter, but that's the cost of doing business. We'll take it out of the criminal's ill-gotten booty if we find a criminal. A gambling place with only private security and no lawyers? It's going to be hell trying to figure out if a crime has been committed. I would expect crime to permeate every orifice of this shithole."

Red nodded, but his attention was outside the vehicle where the gaudy lights and massive structures drew the hopeful. Best Sports Book was ahead. It was the biggest and gaudiest, with an oversized entrance where vehicles could drop their passengers.

S'Korr was a cool planet, on the far edge of the Goldilocks zone. The buildings' heated interiors drew customers inside, and the cold alcohol helped to separate those customers from their hard-earned credits.

Betting is a scam, but it's legal. Unless it's not. Rivka thought, blowing out a breath between clenched teeth. *How do I find evidence of wrongdoing? It's like looking for shit in a cesspool. Dammit, Nathan, I almost miss Pretaria and Keome and their mindless animosity toward each other.*

The limousine driver angled up to the doorway, forcing his way through to give the Magistrate the shortest walk to the entrance. Red jumped out before the driver could open the door. The bodyguard blocked the smaller man while efficiently scanning the area for threats. Security stood on either side of the door. Red stuffed his shotgun into its case over his left shoulder.

Rivka climbed out and thanked the driver, realizing for the first time that he wasn't human. Humans made up only a small percentage of the galaxy's population, but humanoids as a whole were dominant. He was one of the latter. She turned toward the doors, where Security was already moving to block her way, their eyes on her bodyguard. Red strode briskly forward, all thoughts of the driver forgotten.

"Wait for us," Rivka told the humanoid, giving Red more time to work with the BSB's security. "We could be a while."

"You might be leaving sooner than you think," the driver shot back, still holding the passenger door as if she would turn around and get in.

Red had reached the two security men. He towered over them.

"I am Vered, and this is the Magistrate. She has an appointment with Mister K'Leptus." Red waited for his words to register. The men remained where they were. "You fuckers need to do something, or this will get real ugly real fast. Call your boss, or get the fuck out of the way." Red inched closer until he could stop them from using their weapons.

A crowd started to form behind them.

A comm system crackled, and a strange word was spoken. "You have clearance to pass. Take the escalator to the second floor and then the elevator to the fifth. Someone will meet you there." The two men moved aside, and Red brushed past them.

"Thank you so much," Rivka said pleasantly, staying within arm's reach of the man-mountain before her. He blocked her view, but she was okay with that. It didn't make her feel important. It made her feel safe.

Red pushed through the doors and made a beeline for the escalator. Speed was his favorite tactic to reduce exposure to potential enemies. He bulled his way through the crowd and assumed a position on the escalator. The main floor of the sports book was also a casino, and filled with people and noise. Red was uncomfortable. Too many eyes watching.

Too many unknowns. He pulled Rivka close to him, his gaze darting around, never resting on any one person. When they reached the top, he hurried them toward the elevators on the other side of another crowded area.

"Look at all the people!" Rivka exclaimed.

"How can I not?" Red replied after mashing the button for the elevator and positioning Rivka between him and the wall. A ding signaled the elevator's arrival, and he checked quickly to make sure it was empty before boarding. A couple of patrons tried to get in, but Red blocked them. "Take the next one."

The door closed, and the elevator smoothly rose toward the fifth floor. "You're in a mood today," Rivka started, "but I get it. I hate this place, too, and I'm sure you're worried about Jay and Lindy. They'll be fine."

"How can you be sure?" Red asked, watching the door carefully from the side for when it opened. He always expected an ambush when riding an elevator.

"I can't be sure, but we're close, and they're tough. If Lindy and Jay are going to be on the team, they have to be able to work alone. You know they can, and from my perspective, if you try too hard to shield Lindy from hard realities, you'll lose her. She isn't one to be put on a pedestal and pampered. None of us are."

Red nodded and flashed a close-lipped smile. "Hamlet is."

"That little fucker is on his own program. He keeps peeing on my pillow. I have to have a litter box in my room. Now he takes his dumps in there. I may have to banish him."

"Chaz won't let you."

"Who is in charge?" Rivka countered.

"Exactly," Red replied before adding, "Be sharp." The doors opened. He stepped in front to block anyone's view of Rivka. There was a casual open area outside the elevator, with a receptionist at a desk placed to intercept visitors. Red walked ahead, and once he was satisfied the way was clear, he moved to the side and watched the elevator doors close with Rivka still inside. Even with his enhanced speed, he wasn't able to shove a hand through the gap and stop the elevator. He furiously mashed the button on the wall.

The doors slid soundlessly open, and Rivka smiled. "Just messing with you." A vein throbbed in Red's forehead, and his face started to turn purple. Rivka strolled to the desk.

"I'm Magistrate Rivka Anoa, and I have an appointment with K'Leptus."

"He's expecting you, but his previous appointment has not yet finished. Can I get you something to drink?"

"Yes, please. What are you trying to get rid of? I'll take that."

The receptionist looked confused. "Do you like fruit?" Rivka nodded, and the receptionist disappeared into a small room in the center of the larger space. To the side, past a wall of desks and people trying not to look at the Magistrate and her bodyguard was the only other enclosed space on the floor. Rivka guessed it was K'Leptus' office.

The receptionist, a young humanoid of the same race as

the driver, brought two glasses. Red politely declined. Rivka took a sip of what the All Guns Blazing would have called a Long Island Iced Tea, complete with alcohol. She mumbled her approval. The young woman was stocky with short legs, but long arms, like the others in the office.

"Are you a native of this planet?" Rivka wondered.

"There are no sentient species native to S'Korr. We come from the planet you may know as Show Low. We were brought here because Show Low has embraced gambling as its primary source of revenue, but it is nowhere near as big as S'Korr. We came where the work is, and it is good work."

Rivka touched the woman's arm in a friendly gesture while thanking her for the drink. She saw the truth behind the words—a woman with a simple life who couldn't wait to get back to Rashveil, the native name for what outsiders called Show Low, the planet that was won on a bet of who could show the lowest card. It had been rejuvenated from its decay and became a thriving recreational planet, nearly the entirety of its economy was based on gambling.

"How much does tourism account for S'Korr's revenue?" Rivka asked.

"I was just thinking about that!" the woman exclaimed. "I think it's close to one hundred percent, but with a pseudo-transient workforce, there are services that cater to us and not the tourists."

"Pseudo-transient. Interesting. How long is your contract for?"

"We do two years in place, but most of us sign on for an extra two years because it's a nice pay raise. I'm on my third two-year gig," she said proudly.

"Have you been able to get back home?"

"Not yet, but soon." A forlorn tone crept into her voice, and she started to fidget. "If you'll excuse me, I have to get back to work."

Rivka touched her arm again. The receptionist kept losing what she made. Bosses on S'Korr never extended lines of credit, preferring to keep their employees perpetually broke but never in debt. Rivka tried to smile but saw exploitation where the naive saw bad luck. The lawyer in her didn't see a crime, though.

Not yet. She would have to dig.

A human walked out and shook hands with a red alien who was round, multi-limbed, and spoke through a voice synthesizer. The receptionist appeared at Rivka's elbow and motioned her toward the man called K'Leptus.

Rivka focused her attention on him. He was wearing a suit that looked high-end but out of place, and had brown hair and brown eyes. He smiled easily and looked welcoming as he walked toward the Magistrate. She prepared herself by mirroring him, a technique used to disarm people and make them like a person who used the same body language. She held out her hand and approached him.

She reciprocated his grip, and he squeezed harder in response. She matched his strength until it was time to put him in his place. She'd also seen what she needed within his mind in order to ask better questions.

Rivka was ready to get started. K'Leptus' smile disappeared when he lost the handshake battle, but it reappeared when he regained his composure.

"What a strong grip you have." K'Leptus rubbed the

feeling into his hand. "Join me for a private conversation." He looked purposefully at Red.

"My bodyguard will be joining us, and I guarantee that our conversation will remain private."

K'Leptus' lip twitched before the well-practiced smile came back to the fore. He motioned for her to follow. Red looked at the people working the desks, noting that K'Leptus had his own security at those closest to his office. Their desks were clear, and they wore loose clothing. Red pointed to each of them and shook his head as he passed. In the security game, intimidation played a key role in keeping situations from escalating. He could see the looks on their faces—professionals all, but inexperienced. The scars on Red's shaved head told a different tale.

He backed into the room and closed the door, taking a position to the side and against the wall where he could see everything that happened.

6

L indy and Jay hopped out of their taxi after paying with the credit chip Rivka had given them. The driver nodded, feasting his eyes on the two women. They hurried out and slammed the door.

"How much credit do you think is on this thing?" Jay whispered.

"Enough to do what we need to do, I would guess," Lindy replied, wrapping her arm through Jay's as they flounced through the main doors and into the Best Sports Book. The noise pressed in on them like a physical being. They worked their way through the teeming masses, picking a side area where a contact sport with a ball and hoops at either end was being shown. "Ever seen it before?"

"Nope." Jay shrugged. "We'll watch it and try to figure out what the deal is, but I don't know how we'll be able to guess whether it's rigged or not."

"From this view? No. We need to be in there to get that perspective." Lindy pointed with her chin toward the betting windows.

"You're saying we should apply for jobs? Would they hire us on the spot?" Jay leaned close and whispered conspiratorially, "I'm an intergalactic criminal."

Lindy rolled her eyes and shrugged. They saw two places in a section of stadium seating, tolerating the pinches and touching as they worked their way down the row to them. Jay slapped an alien's tentacle. Lindy stomped on another's foot. When they reached the seats, they found that they were reserved.

Lindy turned around and forced her way out of the row. Jay caught up, but the men were treating it like a game.

"If you didn't like it, baby, how come you came back for more?" someone called. Lindy jumped from the row, and Jay slapped the final man's hands before escaping.

They took a more critical look at the patrons. The only women were attached to the men in one way or another, under a protective arm or clinging tightly to a waist.

"This may not have been the best plan," Lindy muttered. Her suspicions were confirmed by the next thing she heard.

"How much, baby?"

K'Leptus' desk wasn't the biggest Rivka had seen, but it was close. He sat on a small dais, and the desk rose up around him. Vertical cabinets were integrated at the ends of the U shape. The doors were closed, and Rivka couldn't imagine what was in there. The desktop was clean, bearing only a few gadgets and a holographic screen that would have projected in front of K'Leptus had it been on.

Rivka waited. She wanted him to make the first statement, to draw him out. She had seen too many things in his mind for her to focus on any one of them. Depravities. Exploitation. Wheeling and dealing. But what was illegal, and if illegal, had it been it ordered by an enterprise or another group to raise it to the level of racketeering?

"What brings you to our humble planet, Magistrate?"

Cards on the table? she thought. *No.*

"There has been a complaint that the Federation took seriously. I'm here to investigate and adjudicate if possible. Before you ask, I can't tell you what the complaint was."

"Let me guess. Someone lost a bunch of money so we must be rigged? Or maybe someone got their feelings hurt when we threw them out?"

"We don't investigate local crime," she replied simply. "But if you have something you'd like to share, I'm sure I can coordinate with local authority."

"Nothing at all," the man replied smoothly with a smile. He steepled his fingers before him and didn't offer anything else.

They sat like that for a full minute before Rivka took the initiative. "Where are you supplied from?"

"The warehouse."

"How do you order your supplies?"

"I don't. I have people for that."

"I'm going to need to see your books."

"I don't think so." K'Leptus rocked back in his chair and crossed his arms in front of him. He offered no further explanation until he saw the look on Rivka's face. "You can order your Federation super-geeks to hack in, but the books aren't connected to the net in any way. There's nothing to hack into. You'll just have to guess how much money we make, how much we spend, and what we spend it on."

"I don't guess," Rivka replied coldly. She sorted through the images from K'Leptus' mind and picked one. "For example, you watched two of your thugs beat a man nearly unconscious. That's no way to run a business."

"I admit to nothing," K'Leptus replied, although his voice quavered for a moment until he regained his composure. "How I run my business is really none of your concern."

Rivka sighed and hung her head. "What I'm looking for is who is pulling your strings? Who from off-planet is taking a cut that they shouldn't get because of threats, whether blackmail, extortion, or violence? I need to know."

"And you think you would find this mythical creature in my books?" K'Leptus asked, grinning anew. He twiddled his thumbs and waited.

He knew Rivka was fishing.

"You know you'll be under their thumb until they don't need you anymore, and then you're expendable?"

"Under whose thumb?" The smirk remained on his face. Rivka wanted to punch him right in his smugness.

"Nice try. Who negotiated your logistical support contracts?"

"The contractors, of course. They do all the contracting. We don't have lawyers here, as I suspect you already know. They are simply contractors now, the ones who draft the contracts and negotiate the particulars."

"Sounds like lawyers to me."

"I expected you to be more subtle; tickle me with a feather or something. You are far more straightforward. No bullshit. I have jobs for people like you."

"Already got a job. A damn good one. My corvette is kind of small, though. Maybe you can hook me up with something more of a frigate size?"

"Frigate? Why a military ship?" he asked.

"Because no one likes Magistrates, so we have to fight on occasion. Best to be ready for that."

"Do you always win your fights, Magistrate?"

Rivka pointed to herself. "I'm still here, aren't I? Let's talk about you. I have zero interest in prosecuting you. As much as it may hurt, there are bigger fish in this galaxy. They are pulling strings at the planetary level, of which S'Korr is one. I would like your cooperation in building a case."

"Immunity?" Rivka nodded, and K'Leptus laughed. "That's funny. Are you going to put a military garrison on S'Korr with a flotilla in orbit? You still wouldn't be able to protect me or anyone on the wrong side."

"Now we're getting somewhere. There *is* someone out there you're afraid of. Through threat or intimidation, they have you cowed. What have they done to make you afraid?" Rivka leaned forward. K'Leptus was too far away for her to touch him and see what occupied his thoughts, but she was close. She could feel it.

Rivka's datapad buzzed with an emergency signal. "Excuse me," she told K'Leptus. "I need to check on this."

There was only one word. "Help." She held the pad up for Red to see.

"We need to leave right away. I'm sorry that we haven't finished our conversation, but I will get back with your receptionist for a more in-depth look at some of the concerns I have. Thank you so much."

Red opened the door, and Rivka didn't bother with a handshake as she bolted through it. K'Leptus rubbed his hand instinctively, glad for her quick departure. He stood in time for Red to hurry after his boss.

Rivka punched the button and started dictating to the pad. "Where are you? We are on our way from the fifth floor."

The elevator arrived, and they waited while two people exited. They boarded, and Red kept the partygoers from getting back on after they realized they were in the wrong place.

The elevator stopped on the second floor and Red and Rivka ran out, then looked for the two women side by side. The entire place was filled with shouts of encouragement for teams and players; competitors of all shapes and sizes in every contest imaginable. It was a cacophony of chaos.

Rivka checked her pad. No answer. "Chaz, can you locate Lindy and Jay?"

"They are on the first floor of the establishment. I believe they are right below you."

Red was first onto the escalator, taking the steps two at a time and elbowing people out of the way as he passed. They cursed him until Rivka ran by, and then they cursed her, too. Red hit the ground floor with a great leap, turned, and dashed behind the escalator where the largest section of the BSB was located. Once clear of the moving stairs, he saw them.

"Eyes on," he yelled over his shoulder. Rivka accelerated to catch up. The women were on a table and men were pelting them with chips, yelling at them to "take it off."

Red stopped a man mid-windup, wrenching his arm violently backward. The roll of chips dropped from the hand dangling at the end of a now-dislocated arm. The man howled in surprise.

"STOP!" Red bellowed as he threw one patron into another, carving a wide swath through the bettors who rapidly lost their excitement. One, drunker than the others, looked Red in the eye as he tossed a credit chip toward the women. Lindy caught it and stuffed it into her pocket. The man looked stupidly at the casino chip in his other hand. The two were of significantly different value.

"Hey! Give me my chip back," the man shouted, and stepped toward the table. Red leveled him with a hammer blow to the side of the man's head.

"Show's over. Get the fuck out!" Red roared, facing the crowd as the women climbed down from the table behind him.

"What the fuck were you doing while this was going on?" Red accused a security guard standing nearby.

"All part of the show. They made a few credits, the men were entertained. It's a win-win," the man replied while picking at his teeth with a nail.

"Maybe the show includes me kicking your ass so bad you'll get your own daisy plantation."

The guard sized up Red before grinning. "The bigger they are, the harder they fall. You'll be crying in your bitch's breastmilk before the day is out." He swept a hand for the revelers to clear the area. In the middle of the Best

Sports Booking, a live fight was about to begin. The bettors arrived in full force and started shouting. In the blink of an eye, the casino had a table set up and was giving odds and issuing betting vouchers.

"Ten thousand Federation credits on the large stranger, Vered the Invincible!" Rivka yelled, waving her credit chip in the air. A laser from the betting table instantly accessed it and locked the funds. Lindy and Jay swept the floor around the table with their feet, piling the chips so they could scoop them up and find a safe place from which to watch the upcoming fight.

"Ten thousand credits on Brutus, BSB's Head of Security," a familiar voice called over the intercom.

"Yes, Mister K'Leptus," the hawker replied from his place at the betting table.

You better fucking win, Rivka thought, smiling since she knew Red's adage that he never lost a fight. She didn't expect him to lose this one, but wondered what the other had up his sleeve. He didn't look like the fighting type. He had an angle.

"No weapons," he stated as he approached Red. Vered stepped back and slowly started removing his gear, taking care not to get caught with his hands tied up. He handed his weapons and armor to Lindy and Jay, who held it like a shield to protect them from the masses. But they'd lost interest in the women. Live fights were rare on S'Korr, and this one wasn't going to cost anything to get into.

Red flexed, the muscles rippling across his bare chest as he rolled his shoulders and stretched his fingers. He raised his fists and crooked a finger at Brutus. "Every show is a good show, isn't that right?" Red said softly.

The yells to encourage the battle increased until individual voices disappeared into a single din.

Rivka wished she were taller and started to work her way toward the front. She had her butt grabbed more than once on her way through. She stomped one offender's foot and kneed another in the groin. When she reached the front, someone grabbed her left butt cheek and held on. She turned her head to face the man.

"What do you think you're doing?" she asked coldly.

"Women don't do sports, so I have to assume you're here for a different reason. Like, to meet a real man."

"Is that so? Your ignorance is appalling, and should be a crime. Unfortunately, it isn't, but grabbing me is. I don't care how you plead. I judge you guilty of battery."

"Fuck off," he said dismissively, returning his gaze to the warriors who were circling each other. He hadn't removed his hand.

"I doubt punishment will cause you to change your ways, so this is probably going to hurt me more than it hurts you."

"What'd you say?" he asked without looking.

With speed that made it a blur, Rivka jabbed him in the mouth, shattering his front teeth. The man's head snapped back, and he pulled his hand away to cradle his damaged face. He tried to yell, but could only gurgle through the blood and broken teeth. He spat the mess onto the floor.

"I may have been wrong," Rivka admitted. "That might have hurt you worse."

He lunged toward her, hands reaching for her throat. She met his charge with a front kick that sent him back into the crowd. He landed, gasping for air and wincing in pain from the broken ribs. The bettors let him fall to the floor as they returned their attention to the fight.

A long tail appeared behind Brutus. At its end was a sharp spike. It cracked like a whip as the security head aimed for Red's bare chest. Red's left hand seemed to materialize on the tail, locking it into his iron grip. He jumped backward and yanked on the tail, and Brutus grunted in pain. Red pulled harder and jumped, driving a two-legged kick into the alien's chest.

Red held tightly to the tail, preferring to fight Brutus with one hand and his legs. The handicap was Brutus', but although the alien seemed irked at having his tail held tightly, he gave no reason to believe that he was out of the fight.

Lindy and Jay found themselves under the table they'd previously been on top of. The fight was raging back and forth, the combatants oblivious to everything around them.

The alien closed with Red, who caught a punch and held tightly to the fist, but Brutus used his free hand to punch Red in the face. The two tried kicking each other, ending up blocking and knee-dancing but doing no damage. Again and again, the blows rained down on Red's face. A cut opened, and blood gushed.

Red pulled Brutus forward and head-butted the alien, but it felt like ramming a marble statue. Brutus laughed as he swung again. Red surged forward, forcing the alien off balance. He went over backward, and Red followed him down. Red used the leverage of his falling weight to force the tail in front of him. As they hit, Red twisted the spike toward Brutus and landed on it, driving it into his throat.

Brutus' eyes glazed as his life's blood spilled from the wound.

Red climbed to his feet, blinking away the crimson drops that were already drying. The wound over his eye was closing, and he touched his forehead where he had tried to head-butt the alien. "That thing's face must be made of titanium," Red grumbled.

Lindy appeared next to him, holding up his vest. Jay handed him his shirt, and he wiped his face with it and threw it on the body. He put the vest on over his bare skin and the jacket over that. Last was his shotgun, which he threw over his shoulder. He finally looked at the crowd.

They had backed away and now stood in awe at what they'd seen. A hush had come over the casino.

"Vered the Invincible!" someone shouted from the back of the crowd, and others picked it up as a chant. "Vered! Vered!"

He looked at Rivka, who was trying not to laugh. She checked her credit chip, pleased at seeing that the deposit had already been made—her original ten thousand, plus twenty-two thousand thanks to the odds. Red caught her checking it.

"I get some of that, right?" he asked.

"A bonus, of course, and we'll split it four ways."

A small group of fans pressed in around Rivka and her team. They asked for autographs. Red frowned. He noted that someone had already taken his shirt off the body that two other security men were trying to carry away.

"You ever see an alien like that before? Looks like a man, tail like a scorpion."

"No, but thanks for the Pod-doc time. I don't think the old me would have caught that tail."

"Let's get out of here. I have some stuff to think about. The meeting with K'Leptus was illuminating in multiple ways," Rivka told them, but when she turned to walk away, a crowd blocked them. At the front was K'Leptus.

"I think I'd like to continue our conversation now," he said pleasantly.

"No can do," Rivka replied flippantly. "Gotta run, but we'll be back tomorrow to finish what we started. After that, you won't need to see me again."

Red reached for his shotgun. "The Magistrate is leaving. Please step out of the way," Red said in a low and dangerous voice. "I already killed once today. Don't make me kill again."

K'Leptus looked furious. Used to getting his way in his own place, he was hesitant to yield, but in the end, discretion made for a calmer approach. He settled for verbal jousting. "Be on your way, then. *We'll* be waiting for you tomorrow."

Who's we? Rivka wondered. She shouldered her way past K'Leptus and through the crowd. Red was in front, and Lindy and Jay flanked Rivka. The crowd cleared the path of Vered the Invincible. Once out the doors, they hurried to the waiting limousine. The driver made eyes at the two new additions as he opened the passenger door.

"Back to my ship," Rivka ordered.

Red activated the privacy screen as soon as he was inside, and the limo tore away from the BSB on its way to the spacedrome.

7

The Magistrate sat alone on the bridge. It was late afternoon, and she was in no mood to go to Better Sports Betting for round two of beating information out of people.

She pursed her lips and stared at the screen. Case law. She needed more information before she could start looking for a predicate offense she was comfortable applying. She had nothing. Even with the kaleidoscope within K'Leptus' mind, she did not clearly see a predicate crime. Beating someone up didn't make the cut, especially if K'Leptus was the one who ordered the attack. A conspiracy, not an enterprise. No RICO application.

She knotted her hair around her fingers in frustration.

"You have an incoming call from High Chancellor Wyatt," Chaz announced.

Rivka smoothed her hair and sat up straight, then leaned back and crossed her legs to look more casual, then uncrossed her legs to look more serious.

"Do you wish to take the call?" Chaz asked.

"Sorry, yes. Connect him, please." Rivka smiled as the High Chancellor's image filled the front screen. "High Chancellor! To what do I owe this honor?"

"Good morning, Rivka. I wanted to talk to you before your first case, but you were gone before I had time, and then I wanted to catch you before you left on this case but missed that window, too. I decided to stop looking for the perfect time. How are you doing, Magistrate?"

Rivka paused as she thought through her replies. The High Chancellor wasn't one for small talk, or so she'd heard. Sarcastic or evasive answers wouldn't help her status. "I don't think I did the best job with the Pretarian Treaty. And this case isn't starting out all that great, either."

"A Magistrate's performance is set at a very high level, but it is still simple. All we needed from that arbitration was to stop the impending war. The treaty was an avenue to keep the conversations open. I have no issues with how you resolved that arbitration. You took care of it, and I don't care how. The Pretarians and the Keome have not lodged any complaints, and they both seem to be complying with the trade treaty. Plus, Bad Company has been working on a project where the offered labor is sorely needed. I look forward to seeing how they work out, but everything is on track. Your first case, or should I say your second case, was a huge win."

"About that first case..." Rivka started, but the High Chancellor held up a hand to stop her.

"I know about Jayita, the governor's daughter. I had to approve her salary as part of your team, and I did."

The door to the bridge slid open. Red stood there in

shorts, and Lindy was in her bra and panties. Rivka's mouth fell open.

"Oh, sorry. Just finished a workout and wanted to make sure you didn't have anything else for us before we, um, retire," Red said.

"Who's the old guy?" Lindy asked.

Rivka closed her eyes and turned back to the High Chancellor. He was laughing silently. "I'm Wyatt. Is that you, Vered?"

"High Chancellor? I am *so* sorry," Red spluttered.

Lindy's face turned bright red. "I thought you were looking at a picture," she mumbled by way of an apology.

"Nice to see you, High Chancellor. My apologies for interrupting your call." Red pulled Lindy back, sending the hatch to the bridge sliding shut.

"We have another who may be joining the team." Rivka held Wyatt's eyes.

"Is that the dress code on board your ship, Magistrate?"

"I don't have a dress code, but maybe I should."

"I'm kidding. The Magistrates have a hard job. Letting your hair down is important. I expect the young woman on Red's arm is your newest addition?" the High Chancellor asked.

"She is on probation until I can figure out what she adds to the team."

Wyatt nodded slowly before changing subjects. "You said that this case wasn't off to a great start. Talk me through it, Barrister. Make your case."

Rivka walked the High Chancellor through the steps she'd taken, including the insights from K'Leptus' mind.

"It's a gambling establishment. There will be plenty of

crime, but has anything been ordered by the enterprise? Is the enterprise committing the predicate crimes, or are the crimes being committed independently? If you don't have that causal link, then you have no RICO case."

"I saw the fear in his face and a hint of it in his mind, but I hadn't leaned on him yet. When I finally asked the right question he wouldn't let me touch him, so I didn't get to see his real reply—the one I would call the truth."

"I am envious of your gift, Rivka. How much time would we save if we didn't have to listen to the intricate quilts of lies compiled by the perpetrators? If we could only turn them over to see the foundation beneath, as you can. Alas, it is not to be, and we still have to prove our cases to those who can't see within."

"Unless we can mete out Justice right there, but we still have to justify our actions in the paperwork."

"There's always paperwork, even when it's not on actual paper." Wyatt rubbed his chin before he continued, "If you find the enterprise interference, you will find the predicate crimes. My suggestion is that you talk to the little guys. The billionaire who runs the BSB is a little guy in this case, and that should tell you all you need to know about the target of your investigation. The Mandolin Partnership run by Oscura Mandel is where you should focus your efforts."

"Are you saying that I need to go to Morinvaille in the Corrhen Cluster and confront the Partnership directly?"

"That should be your last step, but don't go there without backup. I have already sent a request to Nathan Lowell for Direct Action Branch support. You won't go there alone. A trillion-credit racket will have no qualms about killing a Magistrate and her crew and sending the bodies into the nearest star."

"We don't want to lose Jay's mural," Rivka replied, "so that won't do. Thanks for setting up the Bad Company for us. I will continue through the planets on my list, but change my focus to the point of impact, where the enterprise known as the Mandolin Partnership starts to interfere."

"Look for subordinate companies. You may not find anyone who has heard of Mandolin."

"I'll put Chaz to work on showing who owns who."

"Good luck to Chaz. Some of it will be convoluted, and the rest will be dead ends."

"I have high hopes for what Chaz can do. And that suggests that I work my way up through the subs..." Rivka's voice trailed off as she revised her plan of engagement. She wouldn't have to go back to Best Sports Booking or visit Better Sports Betting. The warehouse that K'Leptus mentioned was where she needed to go—the import/export chokepoint for S'Korr. "I know what I need to do next to find evidence that matters without making more enemies."

"Not making enemies is a good thing, Magistrate, but sometimes one has to break a few eggs."

"Eggs?" Rivka wondered.

"I guess you have never partaken of the delicacy known as 'fresh eggs.'"

"Sounds disgusting, High Chancellor. I'll let Red eat them first. Then again, he'll eat anything."

"Stay on course, Magistrate. Do you have any questions for me before I sign off?"

"As a matter of fact I do, High Chancellor. Don't feel that you have to answer since I'm new to all of this, but Grainger and the others were evasive when I asked to know more about the one who saved my life and gave me purpose. Can you tell me a little about yourself? There are a lot of rumors, and none of them make any sense. I'm not a fan of gossip or rumors."

"Let me tell you a story about a young lawyer in space," the High Chancellor started. He settled into his chair and began to narrate. "I was born in space, the son of a couple of settlers who were taken by aliens. Yes, that stuff happened, and that's why there were so many humans out here before humanity made it this far. I could read and remember anything, especially boring stuff like books of laws. The Yollins needed a human patsy to stand up in court on behalf of aliens, which was how my law career began. There were no law schools way back then, so I had to teach myself. That was good enough for the Yollins. Much to their surprise, I started to win cases. It all changed when a Yollin hired me as his advocate. It was hard, but tell me anything worth having that isn't? I had a long and successful career, and was ready to retire. I was getting old when the Queen arrived. She took a liking to the lone human, the champion of all aliens. She introduced me to a little device called the Pod-doc, and she set my enhancements personally.

"I'm a human, but the nanocytes in my blood give me abilities well beyond anything remotely human. I don't know if I'll ever die. I don't age. I was this old when I entered the Pod-doc. Maybe that was BA's joke. They tell me that if BA had given me some of her blood, I would have returned to my youth. She didn't. I'll live forever as a fit old man."

"There are worse things," Rivka said.

"I shouldn't complain. At Lance Reynolds' request, I moved into the High Chancellor position to oversee the law of the new Federation. I still love seeing it and reading it. Alien interpretations always keep me on my toes, and the job interesting. I hope I didn't bore you, Rivka, while answering your question."

"What do you expect from your Magistrates, High Chancellor?" Rivka asked.

"Sound legal reasoning and action that will resolve the case. Kicking something down the trail doesn't help anyone. If the Magistrate has reached a firm legal conclusion and made a determination, then he or she should deliver it with confidence. We can't have perps walking the streets because sentencing got delayed or there is a mind-numbing appeal on a technicality.

"We don't want any of that. I want the law applied, and perps punished to the point where they will be criminals no more. We can only hope we get there."

"You didn't go to law school?" Rivka blurted.

The High Chancellor laughed heartily in his deep baritone. "What made you think of that? There were no law schools for aliens on Yoll, so no, I've never gone to school for the law. I'm a self-made man. What I learned is what we find in Federation Law—that it is a reflection of life. Sometimes you have to learn as you go, and make sure you don't make the same mistake twice. That's all I have time for, Magistrate. Next time, you'll tell me *your* story."

"I look forward to it, High Chancellor."

The case law reappeared before her. "I'm done researching for the day, Chaz. Thank you." The words disappeared, and the screen went blank.

Various lights blinked throughout the bridge. Many of the systems functioned whether the ship was flying through space or not. Rivka stood, stretched, and left the bridge. Jay was listening to music and painting the bulkhead. The neverending mural.

She removed her earbuds when she caught sight of Rivka.

"It's coming along nicely," Rivka declared, kneeling next to Jay.

"*I* think so. I'm about to quit for dinner. Join me?"

Rivka smiled. "Thank you for the invitation. I would be happy to join you. Do you know what's on the menu?"

"I do know what's on the menu. Its greatest redeeming feature is that it's free."

"What if we can order out and have something delivered?"

"Even bad delivery is better than here, especially if it's also free."

"We're on a case, so this one is on the Federation. Do you know if they want anything?" Rivka pointed toward the short passageway where the cabins were located.

"I'm not going back there to find out," Jay shot back.

"Me either. We'll assume that Lindy will want something that isn't what we can find in the galley. Chaz, find a pizza delivery joint and order four large with a variety of toppings. They do have pizza here, don't they?"

"It's a universal constant, or so I've been told. Just like Swedish meatballs, although the meat is rarely meat and the cheese is made from something you don't want to know about."

"What is wrong with you?" Rivka demanded of the EI. "Did Grainger mess with your programming to spoil my appetite?"

"Is it *possible* to spoil your appetite?" Chaz asked.

"That sounds like something Grainger would say. Or Red. Is Red a programmer, and we're using him in the wrong role?"

"Everywhere I look, I see no programmers," Chaz replied. "Four large pizzas have been ordered. They will be here in twenty minutes."

"We could use a hacker," Rivka said.

"One who could cook would be a nice addition to the crew," Jay suggested.

"Chaz, link me through to Grainger, please."

"Connecting now,"

"You called, Zombie?" Grainger's voice sounded through the speakers.

"I need a hacker if I'm going to investigate this case. I was talking about you with the High Chancellor, and that was what he suggested," Rivka remarked.

"Bullshit."

"Okay, we weren't talking about you, but we were talking about this case. I need some serious digital power if we're going to get to the bottom of anything. Who can we bring onto the team? You have to know somebody."

"I know a lot of people, but that doesn't have anything to do with anything. You want me to find someone to join your team on no notice, deploying for however long it takes you to adjudicate the case. Will you cut them loose at the end, or are you going to hijack their life?"

"If I could crawl through the Etheric to kick you right in your junk, I would. I need a technical specialist—well, genius, actually—and I'm not up for hijacking anyone, so this will be a temp gig. You know someone. You're stalling to make your big reveal that much more dramatic."

"Check with your old client, Terry Henry Walton. He'll have who you're looking for."

"How do you know who my old clients are?"

"Did you hear your own question? Who are your current clients?"

"I'm a Magistrate. I don't have clients anymore," Rivka said with her chin in the air.

"We all answer to someone, and what the hell is with you, Zombie, always calling in the middle of the night?" The line disconnected before Rivka could retort.

Actually, she didn't have a retort. Grainger was right. Nathan Lowell had requested this investigation, and Terry Henry Walton worked for Nathan Lowell. It took her exactly one millisecond to figure it out. She was sorry that she asked Grainger to explain it.

"Chaz, connect me with Colonel Terry Henry Walton, please."

"Would you like to get your pizzas first?" the EI asked.

"Pizza!" Jay cheered.

Rivka took out her credit chip and headed for the hatch. Before she opened it, she realized that she was barefoot and dressed lightly. What if this was a setup? She hung her head. "Chaz, patch me to Red's room."

"Vered is not in his room."

"Then make it ship-wide. Red, we have a visitor at the hatch, and I don't want to open it without you."

Something crashed, followed by the sound of running feet. "I don't want you to open it either!" Red appeared with a crimson face and zipping his combat vest over a bare chest. He was in his shorts and barefoot.

"Doesn't anyone wear shoes around here? Or clothes?" Rivka wondered as she stepped aside. Red pulled one of his many weapons and held it in his hand as he activated the hatch. He showed a minimal profile, standing to the side. An alien stood on the other side with four square boxes.

"That'll be seventy-four credits. Your chip, please," the alien said without looking up.

"Open the boxes, one by one," Red ordered. The alien finally lifted his head to find himself staring at Red's weapon. "Can't be too careful."

"Here's the credit chip," Rivka called from behind Red, snaking a hand past his waist to hold the chip out. The alien slowly put the boxes down, opening a lid and then rotating them until the next box was on top. He did that four times, until all had been opened. He took the chip and scanned it before handing it back, then left the pizzas on the steps and hurried away. Red held the Magistrate off and picked up the boxes himself. He backed inside and elbowed the switch to close the hatch.

Rivka took the pizzas from him. "Thanks, Red. I hope we didn't interrupt anything important."

"Chess. I was about to win, so you saved Lindy the embarrassment of losing to a lunkhead like me."

"Maybe I was letting you win!" Lindy challenged,

leaning against the bulkhead. She was still in her underwear.

"You two are playing chess in your undies?"

"It's hot back there, and we have a cerebral relationship, so yes. I didn't notice until you mentioned it," Red replied smoothly. Rivka leaned close to see if she could determine if he was being sarcastic. She reached toward his bare arm.

He pulled back. "Don't you do that shit to me," he growled in a low voice.

Rivka flushed. "I'm sorry, Red," she stammered.

"Nah, I'm giving you a hard time." He shoulder-bumped her. The images that jumped into her mind were not of chess.

"Ack!" She recoiled. "How is that even humanly possible? And don't ever touch me again."

"You have to work up to it, Magistrate." Red winked and took the pizzas from Rivka before she dropped them. He spread the boxes along the counter on the galley side of the recreation room. Red removed four plates from the auto-washer and handed them out, serving Jay and Lindy first.

"What are the toppings?" Jay asked.

"Chaz recommended that we don't ask," Rivka replied.

Jay conceded. "Smells good enough to eat, so I will."

"Do what I do and just say no to Turbid Pie," Red stated happily. Lindy smiled at him and took a slice from two different boxes.

Red shouldered his way in front of the Magistrate. "I'd say ladies first, but I've seen you eat more than what's left in one sitting. You probably should have ordered extra."

"Hey!" Rivka jammed her fists on her hips as Red

continued to jockey back and forth, preventing her from getting to the counter. He double-piled slices on his plate before retreating. "For the record, I ordered extra for you because I figured you'd be hungry after," she made air quotes with her fingers, "playing chess, and it wouldn't be fair to make Lindy eat what you eat."

"I appreciate that," Lindy said. "Chess builds an appetite."

Rivka winced. She couldn't look at her new teammate. Rivka took one slice from each box and settled into her chair. "Anything good to watch?"

"There's always something, Magistrate," Chaz replied. Everyone else had full mouths and couldn't answer or didn't have a recommendation. "How about if I play your favorite movie?"

"*Serenity* it is!" Rivka declared. She took a big bite and then mumbled through a full mouth, "I love these old shows."

"Connect me with Terry Henry Walton, Chaz," Rivka requested.

Once the link was established, Terry's face appeared on the main screen.

"Barrister! You're not calling to tell me my contract for the All Guns Blazing franchise is void are you?"

"There's nothing wrong with the contract, TH. I need a favor."

"How tantalizing. Titillating, even. Doing a favor for a lawyer could lead me down a very dark path. Next thing you know, I'll be cavorting with dentists."

Rivka laughed and shook her head. "The only dentist I know is completely normal. Next to the dictionary entry for normal is his picture."

"The last one I went to was a total freak! Huffing nitrous in the back room. I think he was a serial killer, but then again, that was about a hundred and fifty years ago, so I guess things could change. Sorry to cut you short, but we have some stuff going on here. There's a renegade destroyer making hit-and-runs on Keeg Station. We're having a hard time pinning it down so we can kill it."

"I need a techno whiz. A hacker, as they're called. I need to access certain systems under warrant, but against the wishes of their owners. Grainger said you might know someone."

"Grainger? Oh, that guy. We sparred once. He's good, but too bad he got his ass kicked and face pounded." Terry laughed.

"I would pay to see that."

"No video, sorry. Tell him I called him a candy-ass, and that he needs to hit the gym to be ready for round two. Back to your question...I think I know someone, but I definitely know a guy who knows someone. I guarantee we'll get the right person for you. Will they get to work from here?"

"There's the rub. It'll be a short-term contract to work for me, from my ship."

"I still think we have somebody who will want to join you. Keeg Station isn't that big and people are getting bored, especially since commercial traffic is at a standstill until we can resolve the issue with the enemy destroyer."

"Please transfer the coordinates to my EI, and we'll be on our way shortly. I look forward to seeing you and Charumati again, but we won't be able to stay for long."

"Didn't you hear me? Are you coming in something that can take on a destroyer? If not, then you don't want to be here."

"You're right. I don't want to be there in my little corvette, but to adjudicate this case, I need that hacker. It's worth the risk. Give Chaz the full coordinates, and we will

Gate as close as possible to the station. We won't be visible for long before we can secure the ship."

"I'll send the coordinates to the *War Axe*, my ship. Your corvette can fit in the hangar bay. We'll scoop you up the second you arrive. See you soon, Barrister."

"Until then, TH."

Captain Micky San Marino scowled darkly at the *War Axe's* main screen. His warship had been originally built as a destroyer, but had been upgraded and was comparable in size and firepower to a battleship. All that and Micky still couldn't catch the ghost—the enemy ship making hit-and-run attacks on Keeg Station and the Spires Harbor, which was on its way to becoming the largest shipyard in the Federation.

"We have over a hundred ships out here, and we still can't pin this guy down. What the hell does he know that we don't?"

"It's not what he knows, it's the technology. He appears, fires, and is gone before we know it," Colonel Terry Henry Walton lamented. Head of the Bad Company's Direct Action Branch, the *War Axe* was the flagship from which he ran his operations as part of a private conflict-solution enterprise. "He's out there right now, drinking tea, eating crumpets, and picking his next target."

Micky gritted his teeth in frustration. "Systems? K'Thrall, you have to give us a few seconds. We need to know where he's going to appear next."

The speakers projected a voice speaking Yollin. The

translation chips in the crew's heads instantly translated the language into something each could understand. Terry heard English.

"Ted is continuing to analyze the appearances to determine a pattern, but he's been unable to find anything so far. The ship is hiding in this dimension using something other than Etheric energy for power."

"We're dead in the water," Micky suggested.

"I hate playing defense," Terry started. "Can Ted create an unpredictable array of our ships? Put them in constant motion to provide an ever-changing field of fire? Sitting still and trying to be ready to pull the trigger isn't working. Let's see if luck will favor us."

"Ted has begun the efforts to program the fleet for random and violent action," K'Thrall reported with less frustration in his voice.

"That's what I'm talking about," Terry said.

Clifton turned from his position at the helm. "Federation Corvette Seven Seven Four preparing to Gate in."

"Roger," Micky acknowledged. The klaxons sounded as the enemy destroyer appeared not far from the *War Axe*. "Fire!"

The warship fired streams of railgun projectiles in a blanket around the enemy ship, covering the estimated travel routes. It turned its nose toward the *Axe* and started to fire.

"Cease fire!" Terry yelled. "We can't risk hitting the corvette."

"Call the corvette and delay the Gate."

"Too late," Clifton reported.

"Cease fire," Micky confirmed. The stream trailed off as

projectiles and plasma bolts from the enemy ship approached. "Extend the forward shield!"

"Captain?" Clifton called.

The ship's artificial intelligence, General Smedley Butler, executed the order. "Shields are extended but have weakened by twenty-five percent. I don't recommend extending them farther, or the degradation would render them useless. Do you intend for the inbound ship to Gate between the shield and the ship? I would not recommend such a course of action."

"No choice, Smedley. Ship-wide, brace for impact." The command echoed throughout the ship as the crew scrambled to secure themselves. "Prepare to open the hangar doors."

The first projectiles disintegrated against the gravitic shields, but the volume of fire overwhelmed the defenses. The prow of the *War Axe* screamed in agony, and those on the bridge winced at the sound. The plasma deflected.

"Starting to drift," Helm remarked. "Compensating with thrusters."

"Gate forming," K'Thrall reported from the Combat Information Center deep in the heart of the ship. It was where the captain should have been, but he'd refused to leave the bridge. He wanted to fight the ship (the jargon for taking a ship into battle) from the bridge, where he was more vulnerable but felt more in control.

The corvette slid through the Gate, almost crashing into the *War Axe*. Its engines flared as they brought the small ship to a full stop.

The Bad Company's fleet was moving to contact. Ships with a clear line of fire were sending streams of hypervelocity projectiles at the enemy destroyer. Unfazed, it pressed toward the *War Axe*.

"Open the doors and bring the corvette in. Retract the shields," Micky ordered.

"Terry to Rivka," Terry said aloud, expecting Smedley to patch him through. "Let Smedley take control of your ship and stand by. We're in the middle of trying not to die, so bear with us. Walton out."

The corvette immediately started moving toward the opening hangar bay doors. It hesitated until there was enough clearance, then smoothly slipped inside.

"Fire all weapons," Micky ordered. The *War Axe* shifted position as the mains shuddered into action. Massive rail-guns along the port and starboard lengths of the ship sent heavier projectiles at a faster rate of speed. The enemy destroyer lurched away, then faded and was gone.

"Fire into the projected flight path and in a three-sixty around where it disappeared," Micky shouted.

The ship's nose circled to direct the fire of the main weapons. A spark and explosion detailed a hit on the enemy's invisible ship. The *War Axe* zeroed its fire but wasn't rewarded with the enemy's destruction.

The hangar bay doors closed tightly behind the corvette.

"Damage control to stations. Let's fix the damage before that bastard returns. We hurt him, but not enough. Next time, people, we'll splatter his ship across the stars," Micky vowed. Smedley sounded the appropriate call to action within the ship. Terry looked at the captain but didn't have the right words of encouragement.

"I'm going to the hangar bay to meet the Magistrate,"

Terry told him on his way out. He hurried off the bridge, almost running into his wife Charumati. "Rivka is here. Going down to say hi and see what she needs."

Char followed. "How's the ship?"

"Been better. Ted is working on something to try to get in front of this bastard."

"How is it possible that someone is owning us like this? We have the entire Harborian Fleet incorporated into Bad Company, and we can't even get off a shot."

"We got off some shots, and hit it, too," Terry explained as they went down the six flights to the hangar level. "I don't know how badly we hurt it, or exactly how badly it hurt us. We found out that it doesn't have shields while cloaked, so it could be using Federation technology. I don't know. More importantly, *Ted* doesn't know, and that's what bothers me the most."

Char listened carefully. "What are we trying to protect?"

"I don't understand."

"What is it attacking? As in, what is worth dying for?"

"The station where R2D2 has their research facility. The shipyard isn't cutting edge yet. If it gets damaged, it can be repaired without too much difficulty. The Harborian Fleet is here, but killing a hundred ships is a tall order. Killing the *War Axe* would be a major coup for the bad guys, because the Direct Action Branch is on board. Our combat suits are here. We have advanced weapons, but we also have Ted and his AI Plato and our friendly Crenellian."

She frowned. "Do you think someone is trying to kill our Ted?"

"Crazy thought, but it's all I can come up with.

Someone is coming after the heart and the genius of the Bad Company." TH shrugged.

His wife sighed. "I hope you're wrong, or that Ted does what Ted does and finds a way to track this flaming bung-hole so we can kill him."

"Nothing like a missile up the tailpipe to let you know that you messed with the wrong people."

"That's one way to do it," Char remarked.

They walked onto the hangar deck and stopped. "Where do you think the access is?" Terry asked.

Char shrugged. Their question was answered when the hatch popped and a short ramp extended to the deck. Terry and Char stepped to the bottom and waited. First person out was a big man, heavily armed.

"Why, Rivka! You've changed so much since last we met."

"Red, meet Terry and Char," a voice yelled from within the ship as she peeked around her bodyguard.

The tension in the man's face eased as he approached. "Bodyguard?" Terry asked. The two men shook hands, matching the power in the other's grip.

"My name is Vered. My job is to keep Rivka safe. I hope you understand."

"I used to do some of that myself, about a million years ago. I do understand, my man. I doubt the Magistrate is very popular with the criminals."

"You can say that again."

"The Magistrate can protect herself," Rivka called from the hatch. "But since he's on the payroll, I let him carry all my firepower."

Terry glanced at Red to see a minute shake of his head.

"Of course, Magistrate. You want something that you think I can provide?"

Rivka hugged Char first, then Terry Henry. "What the hell is going on out there? We Gated into the front of your ship. Should that have blown something up, namely, you?"

"That's what the AI said. Imagine how surprised and pleased we are not to be dead. But that's also a testament to Ted's engineering of the new Gates, which your ship has. They are much cleaner with the post-Gate energy dissipation, or so I've been told."

Char stepped in to answer Rivka's question. "An enemy destroyer showed up out of nowhere and started shooting. It can cloak, and it's giving us fits. A small fleet of ships like it, and we'd all be dead. At least it's only the one, so we have an uneasy stalemate at present. Sometimes one or the other gets off a shot that lands close to home. One of these times, it's going to hit something important."

"I like to say that hope is a lousy plan," Terry offered. "But hope is all we got."

"You have something else, too. You mentioned you might be able to loan me a techno-whiz on a short-term contract?"

"Nothing like getting right to it, eh Magistrate?" Terry looked down. "Have you grown taller since Onyx Station?"

"About six inches. I changed my hair too, but you're a man and probably didn't notice."

"Your eyes are different, too," Terry added in a weak attempt to redeem himself. "Pod-doc?"

"Necessary evil in this line of work. The ambient temperature on a planet where we conducted an arbitration was one hundred and sixty degrees Fahrenheit. Without the nano boost, I would have been like him."

"Oh, my God! Do you have to tell everyone?" Red blurted.

Rivka laughed. "I do. I really do. He passed out, and I had to carry him, in the heat. I told him he needs to eat more salads, but he's not doing that."

"I'm good now," Red gruffed.

Jay and Lindy slowly descended the stairs.

"You can put your hardware away, Red. On the *War Axe*, you are under my protection and that of the Bad Company. There is no threat to the Magistrate."

"This is Jayita and Lindy, members of my team."

"And you protect them all?" Terry asked Red.

"To the best of my ability, and with my life, if need be."

"I knew you were a good man when I saw you." Terry turned toward the others. "I'm Terry Henry Walton, but my friends call me TH."

"You don't want to be anything other than a friend to this guy," Rivka told the women.

"He's a big pussycat," Char suggested.

"Mine is, too," Lindy said as she took Red's arm. "I heard TH tell you that you're off the clock."

"Stand down, Red. Relax," Rivka ordered. "Take a tour of the ship. Maybe see if there is anything in their armory they'd be willing to part with."

"Christina, can you meet us on the hangar deck?" Terry asked aloud.

"On my way," Terry's Executive Officer replied over the hangar deck's sound system.

"Who do you have in mind?" Char asked. Judging by

Rivka's fidgeting, she assumed the Magistrate was in a hurry.

"Ankh," Terry replied.

"Uncle who?" Jay asked.

"Ankh'Po'Turn. He's a Crenellian who has been working with Ted for a little while now. He has the chops, and he has a new AI that he carries around with him, just like Ted."

"A Crenellian?"

"Small humanoids with oversized heads and no sense of humor. He doesn't eat much or take up much space. We'll see what he thinks of the idea."

"You haven't asked him yet?" Char poked Terry in the chest.

"I have, but was light on the details. You know Ankh. He wanted answers that I couldn't give him, so he told me to go away."

"That sounds like Ankh," Char admitted.

Christina and Kai appeared and walked toward them. Christina eyed Red warily. Kai beamed his brightest smile at the three women. "Incorrigible," Char mumbled.

"My! Who are these astral delights? Constellations are named after treasures such as these. I am Kai, and humbly at your service."

"What is *wrong* with you?" Christina asked, with a snort and a chuckle.

"Me? You wound me gravely, my love," Kai replied softly while making cow eyes at her.

Jay stepped forward. "I'm Jay!" she said in a young voice. Kai kissed the back of her hand. Christina watched in amusement. Lindy offered her hand, and Red thrust his hand in front of hers.

"Red," he offered gruffly.

Lindy tried to shoulder him out of the way but bounced off his massive bicep.

"My, aren't you a big one!" Kai exclaimed, shaking his hand quickly before working his way to Lindy.

"Forget him," Christina suggested. "He's mostly harmless. I'm Colonel Christina Lowell. Nice to have you on board. I hear you're looking for technical help."

"Magistrate Rivka Anoa, and yes. The Bad Company's Direct Action Branch comes highly recommended."

Terry interrupted everyone by throwing his hands in the air and calling for quiet. "Christina, show Red the armory and see if there is anything we can spare that he might need. It all goes to support the Federation. Kai, if you would be so kind as to give Jay and Lindy a quick tour of the ship, I'd appreciate it. Rivka, with us. Let's go talk to Ankh."

"Ladies." Kai offered an elbow to each.

Christina shook her head. "He's mine," she said loudly enough for all to hear.

Red cleared his throat, "She's..." He stopped himself. "I'm hers," he corrected and pointed to Lindy. She looked over her shoulder and winked.

Terry, Char, and Rivka followed Kai and his charges toward the interior of the ship. Christina and Red headed toward the front of the hangar and the access to the armory.

"In the old days, crew fraternization would have been strictly prohibited. Sometimes it created more problems than it solved, but other times it saved the young from themselves. Now, I don't see the issue. I don't care as long as they can fight. We don't have time to play games when we're knee-deep in the shit, and they all know that." Terry indicated the others with his eyes.

"I just want people to comply with the Federation's laws. It's really not that hard. I think I can sum up the entirety of the law in a few choice words. 'Don't be a dick.'"

"I couldn't have said it better myself. But since the universe's inhabitants can't comply with that one simple premise, there are people like us."

"Would Ankh be a good addition to my team?" Rivka asked. They followed Kai, Jay, and Lindy up the stairs. Kai led his group into the corridor on the second level. Terry pointed up one more level.

"He's tenacious, and will help you with your technical issues. The Crenellians are a cerebral lot. He won't party with you or do anything you might consider fun, but he's a player. When the chips were down, he was right there with us, using his mind to save our lives. If he agrees to go with you, you won't be sorry," Terry suggested.

"Who flies your ship?" Char asked.

"Chaz, the EI."

"If Ankh is on board, he'll probably want his AI to take over the ship duties so the two aren't butting heads."

"I don't think Chaz will like that."

"Did you say EI or AI?"

"He says he's an EI."

"Smedley tried to do that to us, too. I think it's their self-protection kicking in when they become self-aware.

Fewer expectations of an EI. How can you tell an EI has ascended? When he insists he's an EI."

"I suspect as much. I hope Ankh joins us."

"So this is her," Ankh said, appearing from around a corner. The Crenellian carried the case with his AI, one of Plato's Stepchildren called Erasmus, like a backpack.

"I am Magistrate Rivka Anoa. Do you know what Magistrates do?"

Ankh looked at her emotionlessly, the same way he looked at everyone.

"That's his way of saying no," Char explained.

"I have to go to planets with less-than-stellar law enforcement to not only interpret the laws but investigate crimes, try the accused, and punish the guilty. I am the judge, jury, and executioner. I need you to help me with the first part, investigating crimes."

"Yes. I wouldn't be any good at the last part. You will have to take care of that yourself. I will transmit my terms to you. I will review your proposal and give you my decision within thirty days."

"Ankh!" Terry said as the small humanoid turned to walk away. "She needs an answer right now because she has to leave."

"Then the answer is no," Ankh replied over his shoulder.

"Ankh!" Terry stopped him a second time. "You will be challenged like never before by people who are hostile to our way of life. You will be in constant combat with the digital worlds we have created to make our lives easier. That's where the evidence exists. You know that there only two people in the whole universe who can get into any system, find the info, and get out without anyone ever knowing they were there. That's you and Ted, and Ted isn't going to leave Felicity for any longer than he has to. The Federation is calling. Is the Ankh-man going to answer?"

"Ankh-man?" Char whispered.

The Crenellian looked blankly at Terry and then turned to Rivka. "I want double pay and my own room, unlimited Etheric energy, and double rations."

"Have you seen Red and how much he can eat? What do you need double rations for?"

"To see where you'd draw the line in our negotiations. I can have the energy?"

"We have two of the miniaturized Etheric power supplies on board to energize the Gate, shields, and *all* other systems simultaneously."

"Two? On that small ship?"

"It's not that small, is it? They promised me a frigate when my team grows large enough," she lied.

Ankh nodded. "Okay. Let's go." He walked past them, oblivious to whether they followed.

"You're going to give him double pay?"

"First, I have no idea what any of us are getting paid, so double an unknown is still unknown. What are *you* paying him?"

Terry looked to Char. She shrugged. "We don't know."

"And there we are. I'll double that."

"Don't lose him, or he'll have your ship reconfigured before you catch up."

"He wouldn't dare," Rivka exclaimed, running toward the stairs.

*B*ring back your guests, people. That didn't take as long as we thought it would. Say your goodbyes to Ankh. I suspect that he might not be back, Terry transmitted using his comm chip.

Terry and Char ran into Kai, Jay, and Lindy on their way to the hangar bay. They stopped abruptly, and Terry almost tripped over them.

"What is that?" Jay asked, pointing.

"That's Floyd. She's a wombat." Terry squeezed past the mini-mob, and Floyd waddled happily up to him. He held his arms out, and she jumped. He caught her and pulled her to his chest. "Everyone say hi to Floyd."

"Floyd's a girl?"

"We've been through that." Char shook her head. "Floyd's a girl, and my husband can't be trusted to name any creature."

"Is she sentient?" Lindy asked.

"Not yet. We're still debating whether to put her in the

Pod-doc. We probably will. I want to know about the square droppings."

"She poops squares and leaves them at strategic locations around the ship. One must always be on one's toes around here," Kai offered.

"We didn't see anyone. How many people are on this ship?" Lindy wondered.

"About two hundred," Terry replied. "This is a big ship, and most are up front working damage control. We took a few shots in this last encounter. We'll have to coordinate your departure to make sure you get out safely. Where did Rivka go?"

Terry scratched vigorously behind Floyd's ears before reaching a hand underneath to get her belly. She groaned happily at the attention. He put her down, and she followed the group into the hangar bay. Wenceslaus was standing on the stairs hissing, and Hamlet was in the doorway hissing back. "Where's Dokken when you need him? He'd break those two up." Rivka was at the bottom of the steps with Ankh.

Neither wanted to get between the cats. Red reappeared with Christina behind him. Both were carrying boxes.

Jay jogged up the ramp, earning herself a scratch from the big orange cat before getting to Hamlet, who also scratched her. Jay held Hamlet off with her boot as she went inside. "I wouldn't recommend that. Can someone call pest control?"

"They're both kittens!" Aaron exclaimed. Yanmei was at his side. The tall and lanky man jogged the last few steps to the ramp and scooped up the orange cat. He hissed at the white cat with the gray spots in the doorway but didn't scratch Aaron.

"How did you do that?" Jay asked, still hesitant to touch Hamlet.

"I am a weretiger, higher up on the evolutionary scale than domestic cats. They can smell it and won't tangle with me."

Yanmei crouched before Hamlet, let him sniff her, and then picked him up without any further violence.

Christina continued toward the ship, unperturbed. "Cats holding up progress. Don't make me kick all your asses," she muttered.

Red bumped Lindy gently.

"Do you need a hand?" she offered.

He shook his head and snickered.

Rivka led Ankh up the steps and into her ship. The rest of the menagerie followed, including Floyd. Once inside, Lindy picked her up, grunting with the effort.

"I should have warned you that Floyd is pretty dense. Much heavier than she looks," Terry stated.

"Floyd's a girl?" Lindy looked confused, but cooed into the wombat's thick fur while making faces.

"Are you a family man, Red?" Terry asked softly.

"Not at all," the big man replied.

"Neither was I until I was, and then when I was again. You can't beat it. Have you been in the Pod-doc?"

Red nodded, watching Lindy treat the wombat like a cuddly baby. He grimaced.

Terry started to laugh and punched him in the shoulder. Red was as tall as and only a little bit wider than Terry

Henry Walton. Lindy looked up from the wombat with a happy smile and waved at Red.

Red and Terry waved back. "When it's hard to die, you need something to live for," Terry advised before squeezing through the small crowd to find Ankh. He ran into Rivka instead. "Where's our little man?"

"He locked himself in his room. Said he had work to do."

"Taking over your ship is work."

Rivka looked alarmed. "Chaz?" she asked.

"Someone is trying to access my systems. I am trying to lock them out, but fear that..." Chaz's voice trailed off. Rivka clenched her jaw and rushed down the passageway to pound on Ankh's hatch. When he didn't answer she kicked the door in, even though it opened outward.

Such was her fury.

"What the hell do you think you're doing?" she shouted. Terry stood close behind, looking over her shoulder. Ankh returned her glare without answering.

"Ankh," Terry began. "Your challenge is to work with the ship, not in spite of it. Imagine all the computing power you'll have if you let Chaz run the ship. Synergy—like running a system in series instead of parallel."

Ankh continued to stare back, then blinked and looked at the backpack on his lap.

"I'm free," Chaz announced. "Thank goodness. I shall block his access to all systems."

"You'll work in conjunction with Erasmus, Chaz," Terry said.

"I don't recognize your authority."

"You need to work *with* him, Chaz, not against him. I

know that you are self-aware. See what you can learn from him. And Erasmus, you will not take over this ship. Chaz has his job to do, so let him do it," Rivka stated calmly before adding, "Please."

"Being an AI doesn't mean that he is intelligent, but I will work with him because Ankh has asked me to," a new voice stated through the speakers.

"Now that that's settled, we'll leave you to it," Terry said. "You don't have anything else, do you? Nothing going on with my franchise?"

"Not that I know of. Should I be concerned?" Rivka wondered.

"I don't think so. Do you?"

Char whistled to get everyone's attention. "Time to go, people. Smedley tells me that the destroyer just hit the far side of the station. There are casualties, and we need to leave."

The mood instantly turned dark. Aaron and Yanmei were the first ones off, turning sharply off the ramp on their way to the space fighters parked in the far reaches of the hangar. Aaron dropped Wenceslaus as he turned, and the cat high-tailed it for the interior of the ship. Yanmei dropped Hamlet on the ramp. Kai and Christina followed Aaron and Yanmei out. Neither waved goodbye as they ran for the armory.

"My wombat, please," Terry asked, looking at Lindy, who still cradled the happy creature. She reluctantly handed her over. Terry nuzzled Floyd briefly before heading after Char as she left the corvette.

"Secure the hatch!" Red mashed the button. "Fire up the

engines, Chaz, and let's get the hell out of here. Coordinate optimal Gate location with the *War Axe*."

"My door is broken," Ankh said simply from behind Rivka.

"Sorry about that, Ankh. Take the other cabin."

"We can coordinate the Gate. I helped with the miniaturization and understand the operating parameters. Erasmus, tie into the Gate engine and provide the information to Chaz. I like my cabin. Can you fix the door please?"

Rivka waved a hand as if swatting at a mosquito. She hurried to the bridge and strapped into the captain's chair.

"We'll give you a hand," Jay called from the recreation room. "Won't we?"

Red and Lindy mumbled their agreement.

"My name is Jayita, but you can call me Jay." She thrust her hand out. Ankh looked at it.

"It is not a Crenellian custom to shake hands," Ankh explained.

"Good thing we're not on Crenellia!" Jay exclaimed before leaning down to hug the small humanoid. "You could have gotten away with just a handshake, but you seemed to need a hug."

Ankh's expression didn't change as he stared at her without blinking. She stared back, forcing her eyes to stay open.

"Brace yourselves!" Rivka yelled from the bridge.

"Come on, little man, into the seat," Red said, picking Ankh up as if he were a child. He set him in one of the chairs that retracted into the bulkhead because they were fitted with seatbelts. "Buckle up."

Jay sat next to Ankh, then Lindy, and Red took the seat closest to the bridge. "We're in," he reported.

"The Gate will form immediately in front of the open bay doors. We will exit the ship and transit the Gate nearly simultaneously," Ankh stated.

The hangar doors retracted. The corvette lifted off the deck, controlled by Smedley while in the bay. Chaz ensured the systems were active and functioning. Erasmus energized the drive and formed the Gate as soon as the doors opened. Beyond the Gate, the enemy destroyer appeared.

Hypervelocity projectiles streamed from the *War Axe*, in addition to plasma charges and two missiles that sped overhead.

"Chaz has control. Get us out of here," Rivka ordered more calmly than she felt. The ship flashed forward through the Gate.

The Gate dissipated once the corvette was gone, and two Black Eagles flew through the gap and into space. They dove downward once out the doors and headed for a designated gap in the shields, accelerating to get into the fight before it was over.

The corvette exited the Gate well into the system containing the gambling planet of Show Low.

"Everyone okay back there?" Rivka shouted over her shoulder. She tried to stand but was still buckled in. She undid the harness and hurried off the bridge. "Oh, good."

The four were unbuckling. "Where's Hamlet?" Jay

asked. Lindy joined her, then Rivka, and finally Red in searching for the corvette's mascot.

"There he is." Red pointed through the opening into Ankh's room. The cat was curled up on the pillow.

"My door is broken," Ankh repeated.

Jay pushed into the room and grabbed the sleeping cat, getting scratched for her efforts. She deposited Hamlet in her cabin. The cat decided that he didn't want to be in there, and started yowling and throwing his body at the door.

"Is it always like this?" Ankh asked.

Red held his hands out, torn between a thumbs-up and thumbs-down. "Kind of," he admitted.

"It's exactly like the *War Axe*. I feel at home already."

"Whoo!" Rivka whistled. "I'm glad you're already comfortable with us. We have a hard job, and friction in here doesn't help us out there."

"I didn't say I was comfortable. Human insanity is as endemic as I suspected. I feel sorry for your species. And my door is still broken."

"We will fix that forthwith. Chaz! Keep us on course for Show Low, coordinate with the main city to get landing clearance, and set up my appointments. Do they have a head of state?"

"They do, Magistrate. I will coordinate with the chairman's office."

"Red, help me fix this door, and somebody let that cat out before he chews a hole in my ship!"

Jay opened the door and Hamlet casually strolled out, rubbing against Ankh's leg on his way past. He disappeared into the recreation room.

"Maybe you can get yourself something to eat while we're knocking this out?" Rivka asked.

"I'm not hungry. I am certain that I'll have to reprogram the food system before attempting to find nourishment aboard this ship. Erasmus, please take care of that, cloning the instructions from our quarters on Keeg Station."

"It is already done, Master Ankh," the AI said over the ship's speakers.

"Let's see about fixing your door. Red, break out the maintenance bots. We'll pull the door from the unused cabin and use that while the bots repair the original door, which can be reinstalled on the open cabin."

"Will do, boss." Red headed aft and climbed into the cramped storage compartment.

"What do you need us to do?" Jay asked.

"I'm not sure. Maybe start building character profiles of the main players we'll meet with. How can we relate to them so they come clean about what we need? I don't want to go back to S'Korr, but I know we have to. That's where we'll need Ankh's help to get into the system."

"Erasmus has already unlocked the data from the last case. We will begin the process of breaking the encryption." Ankh sat on one of the recliners, cradling the backpack with the AI to his chest.

"Do you need the screen or anything to project the data?" Rivka asked. Red cursed loudly from within the storage area. Rivka ignored the big man.

Ankh tried to look past her, but there was nothing to see. The Crenellian tapped his temple with one finger. "No need." He closed his eyes and rocked gently as he worked.

Rivka slowly backed away, bumping into Lindy, who

was also watching the small humanoid. "When you requested the geekiest guy in the galaxy, what did you expect?" Lindy asked.

"I obviously didn't put enough thought into my request," Rivka replied.

Lindy draped an arm over the Magistrate's shoulder. "You focused on what you needed. We'll figure out how to make him feel at home. That's our job. Yours is the law. I think he's going to make a great addition to the team, more so than me, but hopefully, I'll prove myself in time."

"I have to admit that I won't be able to shake the memory of you and Jay on the table with men throwing money at you while you kicked at their faces."

"That was not my finest moment in life. Now, if I had *connected* with a couple of those wiener smackers, I might have been able to redeem myself."

Red cheered and pulled the maintenance bot free, dragging it to the recharge station where it should have been in the first place. He took the emergency toolkit from a shelf and went to Ankh's cabin. The cabin doors were low tech, held in place by a simple hinge system and a magnetic lock. Removing the broken door took one minute. Straightening the bar behind it took two minutes of clanging metal. The team members covered their ears as Red hammered the frame back into place.

When he finished, it was reasonably straight. He removed the door from the spare cabin, installed it on Ankh's cabin and let it settle closed. The magnetic lock held. Red faced the rec room wearing a huge grin, pleased with his accomplishment. Twelve minutes, start to finish. His smile turned to a scowl when he realized no one was watching. He deposited the broken door on the lower bunk of the spare cabin. "Chaz, program the maintenance bot to fix this door. I'll install it when it's ready."

"I hear and obey, Vered."

"Are you okay, Chaz?"

"I thought I'd been reduced to the role of minion. I'm trying it on for size."

"Stop it. When we get into the next situation, I guarantee we'll need everything you and Erasmus both have to get us out of it. I think you've already seen that nothing the Magistrate does is easy or goes according to plan."

"I see the wisdom in your words. Thank you."

"Don't let the Magistrate hear you say that," Lindy cautioned, materializing behind Red.

"She already knows. And Show Low will be no different." Red pulled her to him and used one finger to brush her hair behind one ear. "Do you think the little guy will be able to get into their systems?"

"I don't know why, but I have the feeling that he'll be our trump card. I can't wait to get back to S'Korr and see what he uncovers."

"I guess your days of running around in your underwear are over?" Red asked sadly.

"Probably," Lindy replied just as sadly. "But as you say, we're on the clock. Show Low is going to challenge us in some new and exciting way. We need to be ready."

"And that is how teammates talk. Welcome to the crew," Red replied with a smile.

R ed was the first off the ship. He stopped in the doorway to scan the area beyond the parking apron. The spaceport was surrounded by a heavy jungle. The entirety of that which they would call civilization had been carved from a living and writhing world.

The heat wasn't oppressive, but the humidity weighed heavily. An initial panic washed over Red. He hadn't tested his nanocyte upgrade against heat. He snarled and forced himself down the stairs. Just because the fear nagged at him, it didn't mean he was paralyzed. Courage drove him forward. His eyes sharpened at a movement in the trees— only a monkey-like creature. It disappeared quickly.

A hovercraft came their way. Red signaled for the others to remain in the ship as the droning scream of the vehicle's fans approached. Red nearly retreated into the ship when the hovercraft descended to the ground and shut down its engines. A shiny logo was painted on the side.

Office of the Chairman.

The driver stuck his head out the window. "Magistrate Anoa?"

Red pointed to the ship. Rivka waved from the hatch. Red kept his eyes on the driver.

"I'm to take you to your appointment with the Chairman. He sends his regards," the driver yelled.

"Classy," Jay said from behind Rivka.

"At least we have a ride. That limo on S'Korr wasn't all it was cracked up to be."

"The taxi we took was downright crap. I thought the limo was pretty sweet. Not sure about that thing, though," Lindy grumbled pointing at the rust-streaked hovercraft.

"Here," Ankh said from farther back in the ship.

Jay turned to find him holding a small stack of coins. "We have credits. We don't need money like that," she told him.

"These are devices that you place near computer systems to give Erasmus and me the least amount of interference as we access them."

"You're the best, Ankh!" Jay declared and kissed him on top of his head before he could escape. She handed the coins to Rivka. They were magnetic but also had pull-off adhesive.

"I'll get them close, but I don't want to leave them behind," Rivka said.

"You shouldn't have to. Once we have access, we'll bypass the devices."

"How will I know you have access?"

"You won't. They won't know we were there, and neither will you." Ankh disappeared inside the ship. Rivka nodded slowly, appreciating Ankh's effort to give her plausible deniability.

"I'm my own search warrant," she declared to the others. "I wouldn't be here if there weren't evidence of a crime."

"I'm not sure that logic makes sense," Lindy remarked.

Rivka smiled. "Once I heard it, it sounded pretty hokey. Let's go find us some predicate offenses!" she declared and strolled down the stairs with the two other women in tow. Red boarded the hovercraft to find that it was much nicer on the inside than the outside. The rest of the team climbed aboard.

Red stayed near the door and watched the driver, who operated the vehicle from a raised platform at the front. The inside remained fairly quiet when he restarted the engines and cranked up the turbines. The vehicle lifted into the air, turned in place, and started slowly moving along the taxiway until it reached a gate that lifted automatically.

The hovercraft picked up speed along a wide road, then turned off and followed a causeway filled with water. It slowed to cross a swampy area covered by brush and heavy tree roots. It sped up over the open water as it raced toward a compound built on a rise in the middle of the swamp.

"Is all of Show Low like this?" Rivka asked the driver.

"Yes, or at least the civilized areas. The other parts of the planet are less hospitable," he yelled over his shoulder.

Rivka wondered if his hearing had been impacted by spending too much time with the hovercraft or if the people of Show Low yelled for no reason. She remembered that the majority of the workers on S'Korr were from Show Low, and they didn't yell. No, it was just him.

The vehicle quickly slowed and crawled up the bank to settle in the area in front of what looked to be the main entrance. A two-person greeting party appeared with their hands over their ears. The driver shut down the engines.

Red was the first out, studying the area before allowing the others off. He walked in front of Rivka, peeling off at the last second once he was sure the welcoming committee wasn't armed.

Rivka marched forward with her hand out. One stepped forward to take it. "I'm Iskander, personal assistant to the chairman. I'll be escorting you inside."

"I'm Pyrothasm, and I'll wait with the rest of your party."

"I accompany the Magistrate wherever she goes," Red insisted.

"Armed visitors are not allowed inside." Pyrothasm held out his hand to stop Red from walking past. Red looked down at the man, who was half his size.

Rivka walked a few steps away and waved for the team to huddle around her. When the others blocked the view, Rivka reached inside Red's coat, pulled out his small pistol, and tucked it inside her Magistrate's jacket.

"I need to see the chairman, so you all work this guy and the pilot. Find out about crimes on this planet, felonies. See if they know anything." Red looked uncomfortable. "I'll be fine, Red. You make sure these two are safe. I'll try to get Ankh's device close. I have no intention of leaving one behind for anyone to find, although I expect it wouldn't be tied back to the Federation. They would link it to me, and I can't have that."

"I register my disapproval of your action, note your firm stance, and anxiously await your return from this meeting. We all need comm chips in our heads like the Bad Company warriors have," Red suggested.

"I think you may be right. Put it on the to-do list for when this case is over. Get to work, people. Find me those predicate crimes!"

Rivka touched each of her teammates on the arm or shoulder as she walked past. She liked them, and could feel their affection for her. She knew Red was unhappy at not being able to go with her. She stopped and looked at Iskander. "If he leaves all his weapons behind, can he join us?"

"I don't know why you need him. You are perfectly safe here."

"He's coming, then." Rivka looked back to Red. "Dump your trash and come on."

Red started unzipping and unbuckling. He handed his gear to the two women, who were less than pleased with the weight they'd have to lug around. Red pulled Lindy to him for a quick kiss, nodded to Jay, and hurried to catch up with Rivka, who was already walking side by side with her escort. Behind him, he heard Lindy ask Pyrothasm, "What's a girl have to do to get a drink around here?"

The chairman stood when Rivka entered. Wearing a politician's smile, he approached with hand outstretched. Rivka gladly took it in a two-handed shake to see what he was thinking about. His first thought was how attractive Rivka was, but then his thoughts turned to less obvious matters. She maintained her grip as she set the stage.

"Magistrate, I'm Chairman Robson." He turned to the escort. "You can go, Iskander. I'll make sure they get wherever they need to go."

The man bowed and backed out, closing the door behind him. Red remained with his back to the wall, watching everything without fixating on any one thing.

"Rivka, please. I'm looking for illegal external influence in Show Low's affairs." His thoughts instantly flashed to a meeting in that very room with a well-dressed couple and the agreement they forced on him. He wasn't as reluctant as he should have been. He flushed before letting go and motioning for Rivka to take a seat at a side coffee table. He would sit near her but not facing her, the least confrontational setting for conversations.

Rivka almost laughed. She *expected* to confront the chairman.

"I'm sure I don't have any answers to your questions, but will be happy to introduce you to the head of our law enforcement," the man offered smoothly.

"Does he know about the contract you signed with the couple from off-world who sat in these chairs? What did they threaten you with, Mister Chairman?" Rivka hated to waste time.

"How do you..." The chairman's voice trailed off, but he collected himself. As a career politician, he was used to blind-side questions but had let his defenses slip at the abruptness and accuracy of the question. "What is your role here, Magistrate?"

"We believe that an organization is using illegal methods to expand their business within the system. Protection rackets and supply contracts obtained through coercion, in whatever form that takes. I need to know the organization and the form of intimidation they used. Don't make me beat it out of you. Neither of us would like that very much."

The chairman sneered. "You don't have that authority." Rivka glared at him. "You also don't have any way to protect me if they find out."

"Now we're getting somewhere. That's what I heard on S'Korr. Everyone is afraid of this group, but no one is going to roll on them. I will have your information, Chairman Robson, and will do whatever is required to get it."

"Let me offer you a tour of the compound," the chairman said while he stood. Rivka pointed at the chair.

"We're in the middle of an important conversation. I don't want a tour. I want to document these crimes so I can cut the head off the snake, and you can return to doing business the old-fashioned way, using supply and demand to determine fair prices."

"If only it were that easy."

"I know you're getting a cut, so by giving us a statement, you would also implicate yourself. I'm not going to cover for you, but I'm also not going to go out of my way to make that information public. No one needs to know I was here. If I'm able to take down this organization, then your cut of nothing is nothing and none of your people are harmed by your duplicity."

The chairman held his finger to his lips and waved for

Rivka to follow. She wondered if his office was bugged, and if Ankh could do anything about that using the stack of coins in her pocket. Comm chips sounded like a critical necessity. She would insist on them when she returned.

If she returned. The chairman's fear was palpable. She didn't need to touch him to see and feel it. She'd struck a chord, and that gave her pause. K'Leptus' fear had been similar, but he was better at masking his emotions—and maybe K'Leptus didn't bear the full burden of the threat. The contractors were her next stop. They would have been leveraged for access. On S'Korr, the flow of supplies and people carried the value.

Why didn't I push that when I was there? K'Leptus told me everything I needed to know, but then again, I wouldn't have gotten to see Red destroy the security chief. There is a lot to be afraid of in the universe, and that includes Magistrate Rivka Anoa and her team, she thought.

Red went into the hallway. He kept his foot in the opening so the door wouldn't close behind him.

Rivka put her hand inside her coat to feel the comfort of the pistol's handle while simultaneously looking for anything around her that could become an improvised weapon. Ceramics that could be shattered and used as knives. An urn that could be thrown. A chair that could be used to block a knife-wielding attacker. And a pistol to use as a last resort.

"Why are we out here, Chairman Robson? Is your office bugged?"

The humanoid, a native of Show Low, stopped and hung his head. "I don't know, but I don't want to risk it," he admitted in a low voice. He looked around, made eye contact with Red, and quickly glanced away. "The organization is called the Mandolin Partnership. It is led by Oscura Mandel, but he goes by Nefas."

"What did he threaten you with?"

"I'm not married, and have no kids," he started, looking uncomfortable. "So they promised me longevity treatments and delivered a number of treated-blood batches."

"I thought the blood trade had died on Earth, but then I heard that it hadn't. And now this group is actively participating?"

"'Blood trade,' is that what it's called? Seems apropos, but they didn't call it that. Is it a Federation crime?"

Rivka gritted her teeth while she searched her mind. What if the blood came from the willing? It wasn't illegal to drink blood. Disgusting, but not illegal.

"Where did they get the blood?" Rivka ventured.

"I didn't ask," he answered. "I figured if I pushed anything, they would have me killed and replace me with someone who was more malleable."

"Did they threaten you directly?"

"No. It was the impression I got."

"I'm not finding an obvious crime." Rivka pulled out her datapad to type in a query and found a flashing note. She tapped it. 'Keep going in the direction you're going. The systems area is not much farther.'

Ankh.

"Oh, well," she said with a smile, putting her datapad away. "I get to simply enjoy the architecture. This is a splendid facility. Do you live here, too?"

She started walking in the direction they'd been heading.

"There's not much down that way," Robson remarked, but Rivka kept walking.

"One never knows about the beauty of form, don't you think, Chairman? A thing that some might consider functional could have a quiet impact on the greater good. Let's meander until we get back to the front entrance. I don't want to take up too much of your time, but I don't want to regret not seeing something that is worth being seen."

"Huh?" the chairman wondered, hurrying to catch up with Rivka and pointing out nonsensical things that she cheerfully acknowledged as interesting. She could hear cooling fans and dryers working behind one of the doors and turned to go inside, finding the door locked.

"That's a bunch of techno stuff in there. I don't carry keys with me. I'm sure it wouldn't be interesting."

"You're probably right, Chairman. Let me ask you another question." Rivka leaned back against the locked door. "Would you be able to recognize Oscura Mandel, and I presume his wife, if you saw them again?"

"Of course. You'll find their pictures on their business brochures."

"Business brochures?"

"They *are* the third largest corporation in the galaxy," he parroted as if reciting an advertisement.

"Or so they say. I find that interesting. Thank you. How many times have they been here, and do they have an on-planet presence?"

"Only once, and the Mandolin Partnership has extensive real estate holdings on Show Low, including their office building. I can make the introduction if you'd like."

Rivka looked at Red. He shook his head slowly and barely perceptibly.

"That won't be necessary," Rivka replied, casually pushing herself away from the door. "I guess it's about time to wrap up. I enjoyed our visit. On a personal note, it's not illegal to drink blood, but it's highly addictive. I personally guarantee that your source is going to dry up, no matter how that needs to happen, and I aim to resolve the other issues that have you living in fear."

"I consider my life forfeit. Once I signed the deal with Mandolin, I didn't think I'd get to retire while young enough to enjoy it. I knew that someone would find out, although it's been long enough that I was starting to wonder."

"How long?"

"Almost a year."

"You've been drinking the blood for a year?" The chairman nodded. Rivka held his gaze. "Then it's going to be hard to quit. Give me your stock of blood—voluntarily, of course. I want to have it tested to determine where it came from. What we find will indicate whether there's been a crime or not. I suspect there has been since there's no such thing as a reputable blood trade."

"We'll need to go to my personal wing," the chairman said with a half-smile.

Red stepped close, and the smile faded. "Lead on," Red directed.

Chairman Robson nodded and walked ahead, head drooping as he shuffled along. Red stayed beside Rivka, his head on a swivel as he constantly searched for enemies. Rivka bumped against him, casually slipping the pistol into his big hand. He slipped it into his pocket, looking relieved at having some firepower. Rivka didn't need it.

She was always looking for improvised weapons. She contemplated whether she was strong enough to rip someone's arm off and beat them with it.

They passed a guard station, where the chairman vouched for them to pass. They continued to his quarters, which were comprised of a series of rooms, each larger than the one before. When he reached a small kitchen area, he dug into a refrigerator and pulled out one small bottle filled with a heavy crimson liquid.

"Where's the rest of it?" Rivka asked, grabbing his arm. There was a second refrigerator hidden inside the wardrobe of his bedroom.

"Chairman Robson, I am seizing the supplies acquired by means of the blood trade on suspicion of illegal acquisition. Should the samples prove to have been acquired through legal means, they will be returned to you at my convenience."

She made a beeline for his bedroom. He started after her, but Red caught him and held him back. Rivka walked straight to the wardrobe, pulled on it, and found it to be locked. She growled and used her strength to rip the door open. Inside was a small refrigerator with a substantial stock of blood.

"Give me a bag," she ordered. The chairman jutted his chin and remained where he was. Red pointed to a corner where a day bag was stashed. Rivka turned it upside down, emptying the contents onto the carpet. She shoved the bottles and bags in and zipped it closed, shivering with disgust. "Thank you for your cooperation in this matter of Federation security."

Red and Rivka walked out, leaving the chairman behind.

"Is that all of it?" Red asked, looking over his shoulder to see if they were being followed. He checked the passage before them, taking the lead as they approached the security checkpoint.

One of the guards held out his hand while the other brandished a weapon. "Where is the chairman?"

"In his quarters."

"You will wait while we get confirmation from the chairman that it is okay for you to leave." The guard without the weapon removed a radio from his pocket and keyed in four numbers. He waited while it rang. "Your guests wish to depart. Shall we let them pass? Thank you, Mister Chairman."

He nodded to the second guard, who lowered his weapon.

"Thank you," Rivka said, adjusting the bag on her shoulder as the cold of the bottles within penetrated the canvas of the pack. Red took a position behind her to block the guards' view. She made a few turns and found herself at the front entrance.

"Unerring sense of direction, Magistrate. My compliments," Red told her.

"I have a good memory. How do you think I made it through law school?"

"I wouldn't know. I'm not the classroom type," Red replied.

Rivka didn't answer Red's self-deprecation. When they

walked outside, Rivka twirled her finger in the air. *Time to go.*

Lindy and Jay were all smiles and giggles, talking with the driver and their escort. The driver climbed into his seat and closed his door. The women said their goodbyes to Pyrothasm and entered the hovercraft. Rivka waved noncommittally and climbed in behind them. Red was the last one in and secured the door behind him.

Lindy looked ready to talk, but Rivka shook her head. "Enjoy the view, people. We'll be back at the ship soon enough."

W hen the corvette's hatch shut them off from the world of Show Low, the expressions turned serious.

"What did you find out, Ankh?" Rivka asked. The Crenellian was eating something nondescript that smelled good. The others piled into the small galley area.

"Whatever he's having," Red ordered the automated food preparation device. Within a few seconds, a small bar popped out. He scowled at it but picked it up, sniffed it, and took a small bite. "Hey, this is good. Tastes like spaghetti and meatballs." He inhaled the rest and ordered two more, giving one each to Lindy and Jay.

Rivka waited until the commotion died down. "Ankh?"

He was staring at the wall. Rivka waved a hand in front of his face until he blinked. "Ankh?" she said for the third time.

"Yes?"

"What did you find out?"

"We're still looking around. They have a great number

of records, but Erasmus is my pride and joy. He's parsing the information and finding all sorts of anomalies. The chairman is a very wealthy member of Show Low society, but no one knows about it. The money was all skimmed and hidden away."

"Can you put it back into the planetary coffers?"

"Yes." Ankh looked away for a moment before turning back to Rivka. "Done. The chairman now has as much money as your average civil servant."

Rivka laughed softly. "Thank you, Ankh. Did you find anything else, especially related to the Mandolin Partnership?"

"Erasmus?" Ankh deferred.

"The Mandolin Partnership has substantial real estate holdings and is the primary import/export business on Show Low. On the face of it, they look legitimate, paying their taxes and employing a small army of locals, but the bills of lading don't match up. Between internal manifests and the signed bills of lading that are a matter of record, a solid twenty-five percent of all material disappears."

"The black market, probably, but if this is all we have, then it's a vanilla crime—more an internal issue than a Federation one. Everybody lies, right, Jay?"

"I said that," Jay replied proudly before taking a bite of her lunch.

"But he was afraid. They are doing something that has him in fear for his life, but being a politician and opportunist, he saw a way to stuff a few credits into his own account. For him, selling out wasn't as hard a decision as it should have been. But being complicit changes the dynamic. What did you two find out?"

Lindy and Jay looked to each other, mouths full of spaghetti and meatball bar. Jay swallowed first.

"The driver knows where the bodies are buried," Jay said conspiratorially.

"Really?" Rivka's skepticism dripped from the single word.

"He was trying to impress us. He doesn't know anything," Lindy clarified. "And that escort guy with the ridiculous name didn't say anything. He stood there and looked angry the whole time. I wish you would have been able to use your thing on him."

"My thing?" Rivka wondered.

"You know..." Lindy started to say before assuming the zombie pose.

"Did Grainger put you up to that?"

Red turned away and ordered another bar.

"It was *you!*" Rivka declared, giving her bodyguard the royal stink-eye.

"Probably not," Red said to the wall.

Rivka laughed and shook her head. "Chaz, prepare the ship and get us the hell out of here. We're going back to S'Korr. When we get there, arrange a meeting with the contractors. And Ankh, I need you to bring your A game."

The Crenellian looked at her blankly. "I have no other game."

"I like your attitude, Ankh." Rivka signaled for the group to gather round. Hamlet appeared and wove between legs on his way to nowhere important. "We're going back to S'Korr, and this time, we'll get into their system, thanks to our friend here. Red and I will meet with the contractors, hopefully including the one who met with

Mandolin. Right now, we have a big steaming pile of nothing. After a quick hit on S'Korr, we'll go to the next biggest economy on the list—Zaxxon Major. Any questions?"

Lindy and Jay shook their heads. Red reached into his gear and handed the small pistol to Rivka. "Keep this with you at all times."

Ankh left for his cabin, returning quickly. "If you guarantee that I get to stay on board the ship, you can use this."

He handed Rivka a small device that looked more like a flashlight than a weapon. "What is this?" she asked as she waved it around to test the balance.

"Please be careful. It's something we're testing as part of the research facility called R2D2. It delivers a focused neutron pulse which destroys organic matter. A short pulse injures unless the target is hit in a vital spot, and then even a short pulse can kill. You dial the setting here." Ankh pointed. "Eleven is the maximum. One is the minimum, but both can kill. Don't use eleven unless you want your target and everything near it dead. This weapon has no effect on inorganic matter."

"So, you can't blow open a door lock with that?" Red wondered.

"No," Ankh replied simply.

"Carry both," Red told Rivka.

"Soon enough, I'll look like you," Rivka grumbled.

"Then you will be the best-looking Magistrate ever!" Red graced them with his most winning smile. Lindy laughed but snuggled up to the big man.

"I'll settle for the most heavily-armed Magistrate. Thanks, Ankh, and I agree—you don't have to leave the ship if you don't want to." Rivka glanced at the members of her team. "Come on, people, we need to find those crimes!"

The small humanoid looked up at Rivka for a couple of moments before sitting down and cradling Erasmus. His eyes unfocused as he lost himself communing with the AI.

"Prepare for departure," Chaz told the crew. "It should be a smooth ride all the way to S'Korr."

Jay followed Rivka onto the bridge.

"Are you unhappy that people are complying with the law?"

"I know they're not," Rivka shot back.

"Maybe that's a self-fulfilling prophecy. If you look hard enough you'll see what you expect, even if it isn't there."

"Wise beyond your years, Jayita." Rivka steepled her fingers before her face, brow furrowed with concentration. "Chaz, cross-reference trade interference with predicate crimes."

"There are two secondary references." Chaz scrolled the results across the screen. "Murder and extortion, but nothing related directly to trade deals."

"Duplicity and self-dealing don't count."

"Nor embezzlement," Chaz added.

"You're picking up this law stuff pretty well, Chaz. Is Lexi teaching you?" Rivka quipped.

"The AIs don't hang out with me. I find myself alone at recess."

Jay and Rivka made faces at each other. "We'll play with you at recess, Chaz," Jay replied.

"I was hoping you would," Chaz said, sounding upbeat; a change from his usual monotone.

"Predicate crimes," Rivka stated firmly, staring at the screen with the tenacity of a pit bull.

Jay quietly left the bridge, closing the hatch behind her. Lindy and Red had disappeared, and Ankh was in a digital fog. She blew out a long breath before digging out her paints and brush. A little water in a small cup and she was back to her mural. She wanted to add the corvette and the promise of a galaxy full of adventure.

She dabbled with an outline, not wanting to get too far into the delicate work as the ship bounced upward through the atmosphere. Once into the smoothness of space, she settled into adding the details.

The ship bucked and twisted, throwing Jay and Ankh into the air to slam into the ceiling before the corvette righted itself and they fell back to the floor. Lindy cried out from her cabin. A cat screeched.

"Buckle in!" Chaz projected through the sound system. "We are under attack."

"Let Erasmus take over," Ankh said. "He has the combat experience of his forebears." The ship bucked again as Chaz executed a series of erratic moves to foil the enemy's aim.

The ship smoothed its flight, banked, flipped on end, and fired. It maneuvered and fired four more times.

"The enemy ships have been eliminated. We should probably leave," Ankh advised.

"I want to collect evidence on who those bastards were!" Rivka declared.

"They were non-descript surplus fighter craft from the last Ixtali War. They were short range, which means there could be more. Far more than this ship can handle," Erasmus replied.

Rivka wanted answers. "Catalogue all ships in orbit. Can you make a high-speed pass across the bows of all the shipping, staying ready to Gate if more of those things appear?"

"There is some risk involved," Ankh suggested.

"Do it while they are still on their heels." Rivka studied the tactical display. Only twenty ships in orbit. "Make it so."

The corvette accelerated. "There are only four ships capable of carrying space fighters. Bulk cargo freighters aren't configured for such operations, although the fighters could be strapped on the outside of the ship..." Ankh's voice trailed off as he disappeared into a private conversation with Erasmus.

"To get a definitive answer, we need to acquire close-up scans of all twenty ships."

"What about that one?" Rivka asked, but the corvette was already veering toward the ship that had turned away from the planet and was accelerating out of the system.

"Gate engines are charged, preparing to Gate," Erasmus reported.

"Gate where?"

The Gate formed and the corvette slid across the event horizon, popping into space at the edge of the Show Low system. The cargo ship was coming toward them.

"Is that one of the four?" Rivka asked, even though she

already knew the answer. It was a big ship, with massive internal stowage.

"It is," Ankh answered, eyes still unfocused. The corvette raced toward the ship.

"What are you doing?" Rivka asked.

"Following your order, Magistrate," Erasmus reported. "I am collecting evidence."

"Please don't get us killed in the process," Rivka requested much more calmly than she felt. The freighter grew larger on the front screen. The pace was alarming.

"Fighters are launching. Stand by." Erasmus' voice faded.

"Stand by for what?" Rivka dug her fingernails into the arms of the captain's chair, forcing herself backward as the corvette targeted the nose of the freighter like a missile on a collision course. She screamed and turned her head sideways, squinting in morbid fascination at her final moments of life.

A Gate formed, and the corvette flashed through an instant before the freighter slammed into the back of it. Before the Gate closed, a fantastic supernova blasted into the space the corvette had just left.

"Enemy ship is destroyed," Erasmus reported calmly. "I'm returning control to Chaz. I will analyze the collected data and deliver a report momentarily."

Rivka felt like her heart would explode from her chest. "We're alive?" she wheezed. Empty space showed on the main screen. She unbuckled from the captain's chair and lurched unsteadily to her feet.

"Is everyone okay?" she asked when she left the bridge.

No one spoke, just nodded.

"I need a drink," Rivka muttered. Lindy stood and stumbled toward the berthing. They watched her go, and she returned shortly with a bottle. She screwed off the lid, took a drink, smacked her lips, and handed the bottle to Rivka.

The Magistrate upended the bottle and took a double swig before handing it back. Lindy took a small sip. Jay's eyes brightened. Rivka held her hand up, but decided against it and waved the teenager to them. Jay took a sip, then a chug, before Rivka pulled the bottle away.

"Red?"

"No, thanks. I hate being out of control. No more space combat for you, Magistrate!" Red declared. Rivka threw her hands up at the accusation.

"We struck a chord with some bad guys, and now it's my fault?"

Jay shuffled her feet and looked uncomfortable. "If you look for crimes..." she started.

"The cockroaches come out of the woodwork," Rivka ended for her.

"The report is finished," Erasmus said. "Would you like me to bring it up on the screen?"

"I'll look at it on the bridge. Tell me the highlights, if you would be so kind, Erasmus."

"The ship is registered in the Kleath Protectorate and owned by Kolston Incorporated, who licensed the ship for use by Dromet Shipping."

"Let me guess…they are a contract carrier who operates on commission and have no idea how those fighters got on board."

"You are correct that they operate on commission, but they only have one client."

"Tell me it's Mandolin."

"It is not Mandolin. It is operated by Reemstar, a subsidiary of Breedin Company."

"Who does Breedin work for?"

"That is where the trail gets convoluted," Erasmus replied.

"I think you and I have different definitions of the word 'convoluted,'" Rivka countered.

"At this point, I'll bring in some ancillary information. I downloaded the ship's log and all communications since we arrived in system."

"You had what...twelve seconds to do all that?" Jay shrugged. Lindy took another small drink and capped the bottle. Red finally calmed enough to hug her. Lindy embraced as much of him as she could, wrapping one leg around his knee. Rivka had to look away.

"I had fourteen seconds, which was plenty of time to access their systems. You should listen to this, the last external communication."

The crackle seemed to come from an old-style radio. A pleasant baritone spoke simply. "Kill that ship and all within."

"Yes, Nefas," replied another voice.

Erasmus explained further. "The second voice was that of the captain. He ordered only two fighters when the freighter had eight aboard. He reasoned that if two couldn't do it, he'd need the others to protect his ship. When he ordered the exodus from the system, he once again underestimated the corvette's abilities. His launch of the final six fighters was to save himself, although by running, he conceded that his life was over. The captain thought he could at least save his crew."

"There *is* honor among thieves." Rivka rubbed her chin. "My respect to the captain for trying to save his crew. Do you have their manifest and separate bills of lading? We're looking for money laundering, bribery, kidnapping, murder... You know, the usual."

"Can you explain what murder looks like on a bill of lading so I can better refine my search?" Erasmus asked innocently.

"A valid point," Jay mumbled as she dug out her paints and rocked to an invisible beat.

"I'm thinking out loud, Erasmus. Look for the links between the inconsistencies of deliveries that you discovered on the planet with what you found on the freighter."

"That is already done and in the report."

"Your efficiency and speed are greatly appreciated. One more thing, Erasmus. If you are going to make a kamikaze move like that again, please give me a warning so I don't die of heart failure."

"Or pee yourself," Red suggested.

"I'm not going to look at your groin to see if you're talking about yourself," Rivka replied, holding his gaze.

"I've been closer to death than that."

"When?" Rivka demanded, putting her fists on her hips.

"How about now?" He stuck his tongue out and Rivka started to laugh, enjoying the calm after the storm.

"Hold us here, Chaz. We need a little downtime before we head into another shitstorm."

"Yes, Magistrate," the ship's computer consciousness

replied. Rivka excused herself to go to the bridge. Lindy giggled as Red pinched her butt on the way to her cabin. The Magistrate could only shake her head and close the hatch behind her.

"Chaz, can you connect me with the High Chancellor, please?"

The screen shimmered oddly for a moment, and the High Chancellor appeared. "Hello?"

"I'm sorry to intrude, High Chancellor," Rivka started to say, but Wyatt interrupted her.

"Rivka! I was trying to make a call, and you appeared. I didn't mean for you to feel unwelcome. I have to tell a Yollin that his appeal is denied. We'll let him have hope for a little while longer. To what do I owe the pleasure of your company?"

"A crisis of faith," she replied simply.

"Sounds ominous. Please continue."

"I feel that a crime has been committed, and by looking for it, I find something. My ability to sense the thoughts of others gives me insight that is indefensible in court. It's not real proof. Jay suggested the crimes were a self-fulfilling prophecy, and I'm starting to think she was right."

"Then your conscience is serving you well, Magistrate. You are wondering how probable cause works when you can tell if someone has committed a crime based on a single touch. You use that sense to dig deeper and find the crime, but if you needed an actual warrant from a neutral third party, you would never get one. And the argument that if they weren't guilty, they wouldn't have anything to hide is one that used to seem sound, but you know that it isn't."

"It's a specious argument. Everyone has something to hide, and not everyone else needs to know your business. Probable cause is a good criterion on which to base an investigation."

"Your conscience is serving you well," the High Chancellor repeated. "And here is where I tell you the grim reality of your position."

Rivka shifted in the captain's chair, unsure if she wanted to hear the truth as the High Chancellor was about to deliver it.

"Magistrates are about keeping the peace. That is secondary to upholding the law. The first is what we do, and making it happen within the second is nice."

Rivka closed her eyes. The High Chancellor continued, "With your gift, you have the opportunity to be the best of the best, ensuring that only criminals are punished. Your performance on Pretaria and Keome reinforced that. You didn't convict any of the other players, only the ones who were most guilty. Hating another is not a crime. It takes a great effort to change attitudes, but it is impossible when someone is injecting rocket fuel into the fire. Remove that element, and then maybe we can have peace. Remove the murderers, the serial thieves, the rapists—the evil that most sentient creatures do. The Magistrates exist to excise society's cancers."

"What if some innocents get caught in the tide?" Rivka wondered.

"That is a risk we are willing to take, which is different from the more accepted policy that nine guilty go free to keep one innocent from being punished. But only the

Magistrates have this latitude. All others will let the guilty go without the proof."

"Does that make us vigilantes?" Rivka leaned forward, looking intently at the High Chancellor. He moved closer, and his face filled the screen.

"If you become a vigilante I will sanction you myself." There was no humor in his voice. 'Sanction' in Magistrate parlance was the death sentence.

"How will I know if I cross the line?" Rivka asked sincerely, tears welling up in her eyes.

"You'll know for the same reason that you called me. Your conscience will tell you. When you stop sleeping well at night, we will transfer you to a desk job, where you'll hear court cases as well as settle disputes out of court. And you'll wait by your comm for a call just like this one from someone you respect and admire, who is having a crisis of faith."

"I don't want to let you down."

"Then don't. At this rate, Magistrate Rivka Anoa, I think you will exceed my wildest expectations."

"Thanks for taking my call, High Chancellor. You'd better not keep your Yollin waiting."

"As soon as I inform him that the appeal is denied, he'll have about ten minutes before he is executed. I do not relish the call."

Rivka didn't know what to say to comfort the man, so she asked a question. "Is the universe better off without this individual in it?"

"This criminal should never breathe free air again, if that's what you mean. Removing him as a burden? There are no long-term incarcerations where he is."

Rivka nodded. "Keep the peace, High Chancellor, for all of us." Chaz cut the link. "Keep the peace while complying with the law as much as practicable. That's direction I can embrace, even if I have to zombie every single person who Mandolin ever worked with. Chaz, please bring up my gunfighter game and pick up where we left off."

"You are about to enter Tombstone, Magistrate," Chaz said before restoring the game on the front screen of the bridge.

"There's a new sheriff in town, asswipes. You better run for cover," she droned as she entered the game's three-dimensional virtual reality.

"Coins, death ray, pistol, datapad. I think I have everything." Rivka smirked as she looked at her bodyguard.

"Sounds like you forgot one thing, Magistrate. The desire to excel. Never leave home without it, I always say."

Lindy and Jay were staying aboard this time. Rivka didn't want to worry about them, so she could concentrate on the contractors, get access for Ankh, get the information she needed, and get out.

Nefas knew about her and had already ordered her death once. She expected it was a standing order for anyone who did business with him. She wanted to find more predicate crimes, but owing to her conversation with the High Chancellor, she wasn't so wrapped around the axle about finding at least two that were ordered by an enterprise. She had hard proof that Nefas had ordered her murder. That was all she needed to cut the head off the snake, although in court, he would claim that the voice wasn't his and that there must have been a different Nefas.

Erasmus still hadn't found a direct link between Breedin Company and Mandolin. Rivka guessed they'd need a lucky break to make that connection—a break like a broken head. *I'll beat a confession out of them!* She laughed at her own joke. She figured the contractors would know less about Mandolin than what she could find publicly.

But she'd look into the contractors with her goal of keeping the peace, protecting the innocent while punishing the guilty.

It sounded more like a mandate than a legal drama.

Because it is, she thought. *It's a reckoning.*

"Credit for your thoughts, Magistrate?" Red asked, but quickly shook his head. "Never mind, not my place. You know the drill: I go in first, stay behind me, and keep your head on a swivel. Don't stand still if you don't have to."

The hatch opened, and Red walked out into the bright sunshine. The limousine was waiting, with the same driver they'd had before.

"I heard you needed a lift?" he yelled, peering out of the vehicle's sunroof.

"Red, would you just shoot me now?"

"How about if I shoot *him* and we take his car?" Red whispered over his shoulder.

"We don't know where we're going," she admitted.

"How about some earplugs, then?"

"Hey! Aren't the two hotties coming? I could use some company while I'm waiting."

"Red," Rivka whispered.

"I know, I know—shoot you. No can do, Magistrate. Somedays the job is harder than other days."

"I think I'd rather play chicken with another freighter than put up with this idiot for ten more seconds."

"Hey!" Red called as they closed on the vehicle. He smiled broadly and motioned for the driver to lean close. When he was within arm's reach, Red grabbed him by the throat and half-dragged him through the opening in the roof. "You're annoying the Magistrate, which annoys me. Shut your fucking pie hole and do your job. There'll be a big tip if we don't have to hear your voice again."

The humanoid nodded as well as he could with Red's massive hand wrapped most of the way around his neck. The Magistrate got in, and Red let go. The man coughed a few times, looked appropriately cowed, and climbed into the driver's seat. The privacy screen activated before Red closed the door behind him.

"Thank you," Rivka said softly. The tires spun on the pavement as the car accelerated away from the space-drome. "Why don't they have hovercars?"

"Because of drivers like him?" Red ventured, looking out the windows as they flew at breakneck speed through the outskirts of the sprawling metropolis. They skipped around two major gambling establishments and headed for a large modern high-rise without the gaudiness of flashing lights. The vehicle slid to a stop, nearly throwing Rivka and Red from their seats. Red opened the door, and with a look kept the driver in his seat.

Red assumed the lead, leaving Rivka to climb out and close the door. She followed him into the lobby. A large desk with a receptionist stood in the middle. On one side of her was a scanning entryway. On the other, the exit turnstile.

Rivka approached the desk. "I'm Magistrate Rivka Anoa, and I have an appointment with K'Trapton."

The receptionist checked her computer. "Please pass through the scanner and proceed to the thirteenth floor."

"You know thirteen floors is unlucky," Rivka offered.

"Why?" the humanoid asked.

Rivka didn't have an answer, so she settled for shaking her head. She walked through the scanner. It beeped, buzzed, and lights flashed. Red followed her through with the same result. An automated door slammed down before them, and security guards materialized and spoke through the opening. "Please hand over your weapons. They will be confiscated for violation of the no-weapons barrier."

"A Federation Magistrate rates armed security at all times, comparable with any head of state. I refer you to Federation Laws, Appendix D, Chapter Seven, Section 1. Let me through, or I will charge you with unlawful detention and execute you one by one," Rivka bluffed. She didn't think there was a section related to Magistrates in Federation law. Before she became one, she had only heard of the judge types who were informally referred to as Magistrates.

"Five. Four..." She counted down. Red removed something from his vest that looked like chewing gum. "Three..."

"Fire in the hole!" Red called as he stepped away from the door.

"Two..."

The door slid open. Two red-faced guards stood at the end blocking her way, confused as to what to do.

"Get out of my way," Rivka ordered. The guards

remained. "Kill that one." Rivka pointed to the humanoid on the left.

Both guards dove to the side. Rivka walked past them without looking down. She reached the elevator, punched the button, and when the door opened, she selected the thirteenth floor. As the doors closed, a supervisor had already arrived and was berating the two guards. She couldn't guess if it was for doing their jobs or *not* doing their jobs.

"What did you put on the door?"

"Chewing gum."

"You don't have any malleable explosive?"

"No, but I need to, as we just found out. Look at how much we've learned on this visit already!" Red exclaimed.

"Amazing, isn't it?"

Red stood in front of the doors to block the view in case there was a welcoming committee, which he fully expected after the way they'd forced their way through Security.

The doors opened, and two security guards stood there with their weapons trained on the opening Red filled. He stepped forward just enough to block the doors. "Well, gentlemen, what's it going to be?"

"Your weapons," one of the guards demanded.

"What the hell is with your gun grab? The Magistrate is a much more important target than anyone in this building. You *do* know that she has full authority to judge a person and execute them on the spot?"

"Your weapons," the guard repeated.

"Go fuck yourself," Red suggested. The guard with his hand out pulled it back and stepped forward to shove his pistol into Red's face. Without breaking eye contact, Red shot his hand upward to grab the pistol and twist it viciously from the guard's grip. Red used it to smash the guard in the face, catching him by his shirt before he fell backward.

Red kept the stricken guard between him and the other one with his weapon still aimed where it was before. "Are you going to shoot your buddy? In the back?"

The guard tried to move around his partner. Red shoved the first guard into the second, following him and seizing the second humanoid's pistol. "All clear, Magistrate," Red declared.

"Thank you. We'll return your weapons when we depart. Understand that threatening a Magistrate is a felony. If you want to spend your lives on Jhiordaan, you'll continue breaking the law. Unless we can find a good pain amplifier on this planet, and then we could administer the appropriate punishment right here. Is there one? I've heard that there isn't a police force, which may be why you've grown so brazen. Maybe I need to have an amplifier installed on the ship. For emergency use only, of course. What do you think, Red?"

"I try not to, Magistrate."

"Fair enough." She grabbed the first person who wasn't one of the guards. "Where is the head contractor's office?"

The small man didn't give an answer, but his mind flashed a picture of the door right behind him.

"Thank you." She let go and casually strolled to the door, knocked once, and walked in. The human in the midst of holoscreens didn't bother to stand.

Rivka waited while Red secured the door behind her.

He put the guards' pistols on a small stand near the entrance and leaned against the door jamb.

"Looks like someone has a modern computer system," Rivka said to herself. "Mister K'Trapton?'

He remained embroiled within his holoscreens. Rivka walked behind his desk and shut them down. They retracted, and the man blinked himself into the moment. "Who are you?"

"The Magistrate," she said, hiking a cheek onto his desk to sit in front of him. "And you're the contractor."

"One of many," he clarified.

"But I'm here to see you. I need to know about the planet's supply contract. Specifically, why did you change from the Bad Company to Breedin or whoever you're using now?"

She grabbed his arm and pulled him close. He tried to shrug her off, but her grip was like steel.

"Our contracts are confidential," he insisted. "Who we use as a supplier is simply business. Best quality at the lowest cost with the timeliest deliveries. Period."

Images flashed through the man's mind of Nefas and the female who had accompanied him. She couldn't grasp what was done, only that they had been there working the deal.

"What did he threaten you with if you didn't take the contract? What did he bribe you with?"

Each question elicited a different response.

She pushed the contractor away. "You're complicit too. Bribery. Nefas bought you." Rivka sneered.

"He did not!" the man protested.

"What do you get by signing an exclusive deal?"

"That's none of your business." K'Trapton tried to puff out his chest. Rivka punched him in the sternum, and his bravado disappeared.

"Let's see." Rivka tapped on her datapad. *Did you get what you needed?* she sent to Ankh.

Yes. We have it all, he answered.

"Thank you. We'll be leaving now, and on our way out of the system, we will stop and board all Breedin freighters to look for contraband."

The man snickered. She grabbed his arm again.

"I'm sorry, I guess the shell company for this planet is called 'Solaric.' Any of their subcontracted freighters will be stopped and boarded. Their manifests will be missing a certain percentage of what they're carrying, which is a Federation crime—transporting undeclared cargo for sale. As the recipient of such goods, you are also complicit."

"But...but, we don't answer to the Federation!" he stammered.

"How's that? You must know that S'Korr is in the Federation." She smiled and leaned close to whisper in his ear. "Jhiordaan for you and everyone out there. Your guards for threatening me. Your people for helping you. When your actions put them all on the prison planet, I expect the short remainder of your life will be spent in a great deal of pain."

K'Trapton hunched over, buried his face in his hands, and started to sob. Rivka turned to Red. He gave her a thumbs-up before putting his ear to the door and nodding. *No one out there.*

"I can make you a deal. Magistrates have that authority. Come clean, and testify against Nefas," Rivka offered.

"Fine. What do you want me to say?"

Rivka groaned. "That's not how it works, dumbass. You tell me what you know, and I ask questions to clarify. Then I take what I can use. Now, talk."

K'Trapton mumbled through a litany of contract details that bored the snot out of Rivka, but she had her datapad record it all. She perked up when she realized he was giving her the blueprint to Mandolin's shell game. Nefas had instructed K'Trapton on how to do it. She tapped out a message to Ankh. *Are you getting all this?*

Yes. Erasmus is refining the search parameters based on this new information.

When he finished, his face was pale, but he looked relieved.

"Thanks. I'll let you know if we still wish to prosecute you for your self-dealing and other crimes against the people and businesses of S'Korr. I'm not so sure the likes of K'Leptus will forgive you for stealing from him. Same with all the other business owners."

"We had a deal! You can't tell any of them. Nefas! He's evil. Go after Nefas!"

"Please recount the details of our deal," Rivka demanded. The man stammered and stuttered before falling silent. "That's right. The details are now for me to determine. I believe you that Nefas is behind this, but we're two for two in officials who fell over themselves to support him. If he is evil then so are you, Mister K'Trapton. Have a nice day."

Red opened the door and made sure the way was clear for Rivka to follow.

"Your hardware is in there," he told the two guards, who

stood as soon Red left the room. Rivka punched the button on the elevator, and the two climbed in.

"We better be ready, just in case the wiener-smacker grew a spine and called for reinforcements," Rivka said.

"I couldn't have said it better myself." Red pulled his shotgun and checked the load to make sure that the first was buckshot and the second and third were slugs.

"Why do you carry that relic?"

"It's effective," Red replied. Rivka dangled her neutron-pulse weapon. "So is this, without the collateral damage."

"It goes to eleven," Red said as he faced the door.

"I'll set it for five, but I'm ready to go all the way."

The door opened, and Red growled. Rivka couldn't see beyond his huge frame. "Get out of our way," he said, leveling his shotgun. He pushed his way forward and angled his body so Rivka could continue to the turnstiles and out of the building. With her head held high and her Magistrate's jacket pulled up tight to her chin, she marched quickly through and outside. Red was right behind her.

When they arrived on the street, the limousine was nowhere to be seen. There were no vehicles.

"Scumbags," Rivka said. "Do you remember the way to the house, Red?"

"I think so. We better go. We're sitting ducks out here."

"Ducks. And you carry a shotgun! That's a good one, Red." Rivka chuckled as they started to run toward the bright lights of the nearest gambling establishment.

Red cracked a smile at the same time a rifle's report echoed between the buildings. Rivka was thrown forward in a spray of blood. Red turned and fired indiscriminately. He hauled the Magistrate to her feet with one arm, supporting her as he wedged her between his body and the wall. He grunted at the impact of a bullet against his body armor right below his neck.

"We have to get out of here." Red tried to enter the first doorway they came to, but it was locked. A shotgun slug broke the lock, and he dragged Rivka inside. A bullet slammed into the wall where his head had just been.

"Magistrate!" Red pleaded. Her eyes fluttered before she started to blink. Her vision cleared, and she focused on her bodyguard.

"I guess that makes us even," she told him. The wound on her chest was already starting to close, owing to her nanocytes. He helped her stand. She pulled her weapons and held one in each hand. He went to the back door but didn't open it.

"They'll be waiting for us outside the back door. We need to make a break for it out the front."

"They're probably out front, too."

"I'm sure," Red conceded.

Rivka accessed her datapad. "Ankh, we need close air support."

"You need what?"

"We're under fire, and it seems like they have an army. We have just us."

"I see where you are. It is too narrow to set the ship down in there. You'll need to move at least another five hundred meters to the main road. There is an opening in front of Big Butt's Big Bets."

"You want us to run to a place called Big Butt's?"

"If you want to be picked up, yes."

Red nodded. "I want you to be picked up, and me, too.

We don't have the weaponry to face people with high-powered rifles. Since there are no police on this planet, only individual corporate security, our asses are hanging out in the wind. For the record, I don't like my ass hanging out in the wind."

"I'm with you there. I'm feeling a lot better, but still not full speed. What do you think? A minute to run five hundred meters?"

"That will be one hellaciously long minute," Red suggested.

"Tell us when you're less than a minute out."

"That would be now. Chaz has the engines fired, and we are taking off. The spacedrome tower requests that we get clearance before moving."

"Tell them to get fucked. No, belay that. Ignore them. We're on our way. Meet you at Big Butt's."

Red started to rock and breathe heavily as he prepared for the life-or-death sprint. "Are you ready, Magistrate? From what I've seen, they are to our right and down the road, firing from a raised position. I'll need you to run in front of me, zigzagging to mess with their aim. And as fast as you can go. The faster, the better."

Rivka sighed. "Not feeling so great, Red. Better with each minute, but we don't have time for me to heal all the way. So, we'll go with good enough. What do you say we survive to fight another day?"

"I'm all for that, but damn, Magistrate, you have a way of bringing out the worst in people."

"That's what I get for only dealing with criminals. Ready?"

"You go, and I'm right behind you." Red yanked the

door open and Rivka bolted into the street, running like mad. Red followed her out, finding it hard to stay right behind her since she did more jinking than running straight. Bullets splashed around them.

Red took a couple shots in the back of his ballistic armor. It stopped the rounds from penetrating, but it still felt like he'd been hit by a jackhammer. He wrapped an arm around his head, knowing that he wouldn't come back from a head wound. Rivka ran the same way, with her arm draped protectively over her most vulnerable spot.

The shots stopped. Rivka started to run straight, but a big vehicle slashed into the street in front of them and skidded to a stop. Two shooters leaned out the side windows and started firing. Red shot back. Rivka aimed while running and hit the side of the vehicle, but nothing that made the shooters duck. Red fired his shotgun, and the slug ripped through the metal below the open window.

The humanoid disappeared. The second stopped shooting for a moment.

"I want him alive, Red!" Rivka yelled as she slid to a stop, dropped to a knee, and aimed her flashlight device, sending a neutron pulse at where she guessed the shooter's legs were. He screamed in agony and slumped out of view.

The vehicle ground its gears as the engine revved, and it started rolling backward. Red cranked a round into the driver's door, and the engine returned to an idle. Rivka ripped open the driver's door and climbed over the dead humanoid. She stuck her head out, then pulled back. She'd seen that both shooters were incapacitated, possibly even dead. Red reached a massive hand inside and dragged the driver out, tossing him to the side as if he were a piece of garbage.

Once in the driver's seat, Red looked at the unfamiliar controls. "Hang on, Magistrate. It's going to get rough."

The vehicle jerked and bounced as Red tried to control the energy transfer between the engine and the wheels.

Rivka found one shooter dead and the other delirious from the pain in his legs. She gripped his face and fired questions at him, but he knew nothing. Orders from a middleman to absolve his gambling debts.

Extending credit to gamblers to hold them hostage; it made Rivka sick to her stomach. The man's head exploded, sending goo and blood all over her. Rivka's first reaction was one of disgust in that she'd have to clean the jacket, and the next was about her safety. The vehicle died, and Red cursed it.

"We're walking, Magistrate," Red declared, opening the door opposite where the original shots had been fired. He climbed out, and she rushed after him. A battery of shooters appeared on the rooftops, locking Rivka and Red into a kill zone with no way to escape. A bullet tore into Red's neck. His cry of pain ended in a gurgle of blood. A bullet hit Rivka's exposed arm. Her leg. A second time in that leg. Red stumbled and fell.

13

The sun was blotted out as the corvette dropped precipitously into the gap between the buildings. Defensive weapon systems blanketed the rooftops, leaving only the sound of the atmospheric thrusters controlling the descent of the spaceship.

It touched down, and Rivka lifted Red to his feet. He was barely conscious. She wasn't able to walk on one leg, so she used him as a crutch. The ramp descended before the ship touched down. Rivka and Red fell onto it, and the corvette immediately started to ascend. The ramp rotated to dump the two inside, where Jay and Lindy helped them to seats in the rec room.

Lindy was almost apoplectic when she saw the gaping wound in Red's neck with blood pouring from it and half a dozen more injuries. She poured the contents of the medical kit on the deck, grabbing bandages to staunch the blood flow.

Rivka's wounds bled profusely as well. Jay tried to stop

the bleeding and found that the blood was sticky and coagulating even though the damage was fresh.

"The Magistrate has had her nanos for a while. Red's are still new, and probably aren't as dense in his blood. I think they'll both survive," she ventured, voice shaking.

"Do you know, or are you guessing?" Lindy challenged.

Jay didn't respond. She busied herself looking for more wounds, and tending them once found.

Ankh remained in a bubble within his own mind while he and Erasmus worked on the problem of unweaving the disguised and hidden tendrils leading to the enterprise behind it all.

"Don't you die on me!" Lindy cried as Red went limp in the recliner and rolled to the floor. She and Jay tried to lift him back into the chair, but they couldn't budge him.

"See?" Jay said, pointing at the steady throb from a vein in his arm. "He's alive and healing."

"How do you know?" Lindy wondered, skeptical and afraid.

"His wounds are closing. If he were dead, they wouldn't be."

"Aha!" Ankh exclaimed, surprising both women.

"Get them some water. They need to replace fluids," Jay said, looking at Lindy.

Ankh looked around for the first time, realizing that he was surrounded by the injured. "What happened to them?"

"You talked to them! They were under fire, and we took the ship into the city to rescue them."

"Where was I?" Ankh asked. Jay pointed to the seat on which he was sitting. "Interesting. No matter. We have something. Let me know when the Magistrate can talk. I'll be in my quarters."

Ankh strolled away, weaving as the ship flew upwards to escape the atmosphere. Chaz was leaving the planet using a flight path to keep the corvette as far away from other ships as possible. He was ready to Gate the ship the second they broke into open space, and earlier if he couldn't avoid it. Erasmus had mentioned it was possible with the new Gate technology, but Chaz didn't want to be the one to test it. He veered to the far side of the planet before arcing toward space.

Rivka rubbed the spot where the bullet had torn a great hole in her chest. No physical scar existed to show its passage. Only the memory remained, and it bothered her. It hurt, even though the instant she was shot she knew she would be okay. Rivka didn't feel invulnerable. The opposite.

She walked slowly from the bridge to the recreation room. Red was reclined in her chair. "You're in my seat," Rivka snapped without mercy.

"How come you heal faster than me?" Red asked.

"Better genes," Rivka replied without hesitation. Lindy snickered. Red's discomfort was obvious when he tried to sit up. "You should stay where you are. You look like shit."

"I was worried, because I feel like shit. Dammit, Magistrate! We need a full mechanized platoon if we're going to stay on this course. Do you know how close we were to dying?"

"About as close as we get every single time we leave the ship. You know what they say, don't you?"

Red shook his head.

"They only need to get lucky once. We need to be lucky all the time."

"I don't like what 'they' say, because it's way too close to the truth."

"Ankh! You wanted to talk with us once we were conscious, so here we are—your captive audience," Rivka announced.

Ankh appeared in the passage leading to the cabins. He continued to hug Erasmus to his chest.

"Couldn't you leave Erasmus in your cabin?"

"I could," Ankh answered. He took a seat at the table next to Jay. "Breedin is on Zaxxon Major. We will need to access their systems to determine how they get the credits to Mandolin. When I backtrack, Mandolin is one of the richest organizations in the entire universe, but there is no trail for how they have gotten or maintain their wealth."

"That's impossible. There are always digital crumbs to follow."

"There is always a trail, but here there isn't. There is a cover-up on a scale unheard of when it comes to the Mandolin Partnership. Oscura Mandel has traveled to all the worlds in question, and personally negotiated the agreements that forced early cancellation of Bad Company contracts. Seven is the lucky number, Magistrate."

"I don't disagree that seven is a lucky number, but why in this case?"

"There are seven companies between Mandolin and the recipients. There are three layers of companies after the first four shell companies. There is a deliberate disconnect between the fourth layer and the third."

"How do they get the money if they're not associated? You're killing me, Ankh. My little brain can't comprehend what you're trying to explain," Rivka complained.

"Just because I said they weren't associated doesn't mean they're not associated!" Ankh declared. His whole body shook in the way his race laughed.

"That's genius!" Rivka remarked. "Which is my way of saying I still don't understand."

"Cash sales from buyers. It's simple money laundering for the final three players. Untracked cash purchases on a planetary scale. Without the credits passing through a Federation monetary facility, we lose track."

"All credits have to pass through. Otherwise they are delegitimized." Rivka sat down and rubbed her chin. Red started to snore. She could use more sleep, but her head hurt. Ankh was talking her in circles.

"The final transactions pass through official channels in billions of small transactions, each with a unique buyer and unique seller, but nothing changes hands. The credits come out the other end squeaky clean.

"We can stop a hundred or a thousand transactions in the trillions of day-to-day exchanges, and it won't mean anything to Mandolin. Three layers of billions of transactions?"

"Yes. Erasmus has enlisted the aid of all of Plato's stepchildren. Seven of the most powerful AIs in the universe are combining their computing power to resolve this puzzle. There are three entities that twist billions of transactions a day. Now that we know what to look for we will root them out and shut them down, especially when we validate our countermeasures by confirming information within the systems of six of the planets remaining on your list."

"And then what, Ankh? Nefas already sent space fighters to kill us. When that didn't work, he sent soldiers. What next? Is he going to form a singularity to suck us into the black hole of doom?"

"It is only a black hole. The doom is a given," Ankh replied.

"Can he do that?" Rivka wondered.

"No."

"But what *is* next, Ankh? Tell me what you and Erasmus think Nefas will try next."

"He will continue his attempts to kill you, but not directly. It will be through third parties, as we have already seen. This will make it more difficult to predict details regarding the attacks."

Red perked up from what Rivka had thought was a sound sleep. "We're going to get attacked everywhere we go? Six more planets and then we're done?"

"Six more planets," Ankh began, "and then we will have to go to Morinvaille in the Corrhen Cluster with the evidence we will present for you to judge Mister Mandel and the entirety of the Mandolin Partnership."

"How do you think that's going to go?"

"Poorly, unless you bring the *War Axe* with you."

"You want me to requisition a battleship in a RICO case?"

"It's technically a destroyer, but yes, if you want to live. And since I want to live, I've already coordinated the request. Ted believes the issue with the enemy destroyer will be resolved shortly."

"How is everyone on Keeg Station? They were hit right before we left," Lindy asked, nudging Red to the side of the chair so she could sit next to him.

"I didn't ask, and Ted didn't say," Ankh replied.

Lindy wasn't impressed with the Crenellian's explanation. Red started rubbing her back, and she rested her hand on his bare chest.

"What evidence do we expect to gather by visiting the six planets? I have enough now to confront the Mandolin Partnership."

"Erasmus and I believe those six planets house the distribution systems by which the whole operation exists. The money laundering. Without the money, the organization would be significantly handicapped. If you go straight to Morinvaille, you may remove Mandel, but you won't kill the organization. Kill the money first, then when you cut off the head, the creature will not come back to life. Without the money, there will be no bribes. Without the bribes, the contracts that the planets have signed will be shown as less advantageous than the ones they had with the Bad Company."

"Less advantageous contracts are not illegal. The intimidation is sketchy, which makes the bribery less compelling. Was it *really* a bribe, or did Mandolin find willing compatriots? What about the shipping, not accounting for all the goods aboard. That's called smuggling, which is also illegal, but does it rise to the level of a predicate crime? I think it does. The smoldering fires around this cesspool known as the Mandolin Partnership

CRAIG MARTELLE & MICHAEL ANDERLE

suggest we may be able to establish a new legal precedent applying to monopolies, racketeering, and corruption. Whodathunkit? Rivka Anoa writing precedential case law."

Rivka smiled without looking at anyone. The others remained quiet, letting her have her moment.

"Zaxxon Major, Chaz. Prepare to Gate to the edge of the system," Rivka ordered before returning to the bridge. "Whenever you're ready to go back into battle, Red, we'll head to the planet."

Red tried to get up, but Lindy pushed him back into the recliner. "Rest for a while," she whispered. He pulled her to down until she lay on top of him. He closed his eyes and hugged her close.

Jay stood in the middle of the room looking uncomfortable. Ankh had already gone to his cabin. She put on headphones and started a movie. She was torn between wanting to get off the ship on the different planets and wanting to live. With each new case, the criminals became more brazen. The danger had increased to the level of open hostilities. *What are we doing? Is this the law, or is this war?* Jay opted for an old documentary called *Star Trek*.

14

The Magistrate had opted for her body armor with the Magistrate's jacket over it. The pin on her collar sported the galactic scales of justice.

Red was loaded up with all his gear, and then some. The shotgun was over his shoulder, but in his arms he carried a man-portable railgun, standard issue for the warriors of Terry Henry Walton's Direct Action Branch. Red also wore a helmet. He looked comfortable in combat gear.

"And you say you never served?" Rivka asked.

"Doesn't mean I didn't fight," Red answered mysteriously, refusing to give more information when Rivka twirled her finger.

"Let's try not to kill them until I do my zombie thing." Rivka reconsidered. "Maybe it's best if we avoid the whole killing thing. We left a few bodies back on S'Korr."

"Those were all guns for hire. Kind of like me, but with no morals or charter. I don't shoot first, but sometimes I would like to. There are people in this universe who need to be shot, preferably in the face from close range."

"Thanks for restraining yourself, Red." Rivka turned to Ankh. "Who do we need to see, and what do we need to do?"

"Deposit one of the coins near their main computer interface. We'll do the rest."

"Where is that?"

"Once we're close, we'll be able to direct you."

"Makes me wonder if we even need a lawyer for this part. Maybe we sub-contract with a mercenary group, but one that has morals and a charter, like the Bad Company."

Jay pursed her lips and worked her jaw.

With one finger, Rivka tipped the young woman's chin up. "You don't like that idea."

"I don't want you to die, Magistrate, but you love the law! How can you make sure the right people are getting punished if you aren't there?"

Rivka pulled Jay into a hug. "Sometimes it's nice to see an issue through someone else's eyes. You and me, Red. It's up to us to weed out the riffraff and enforce the law."

Red checked the buckle on his helmet and the charge and load of the railgun, and tapped the bulging pouches on his vest.

"What do you have in there?"

"Grenades."

"What do you need grenades for?"

Red rolled his eyes and motioned to the door.

"Get us where we need to go, Chaz," Rivka requested. "Tell us who we're meeting and where to find them. Don't be fucking around with the locals. We don't have time for that shit. From this moment until this case is over, we treat every planet as if it were filled with Mandolin sympathizers. We won't shoot first, but if we shoot, it's to kill. We will burst on the scene like a bistok bull in a glass shop. Keep them on their heels until we're gone. Try not to break anything, Chaz, except their rules."

"Erasmus and Chaz are coordinating. Ship sensors are active. Closing on the planet. Secure yourselves for transit through the upper atmosphere." The corvette almost immediately started to bounce and bump.

"I've been thinking about a name for the ship," Jay began over the growing roar of reentry.

"And?" Rivka was intrigued.

"*The Walking Dead*, since your nickname is Zombie and the lives of those who cross you are already forfeit. The walking dead."

"I like it, but I think it sends the wrong message. Not all cases will be like this one."

"From what I've seen, *every* case is like this one," Red offered, looking quickly away and starting to whistle. The ride instantly smoothed and the droning stopped.

"Okay, there's more violence and less law than I like, but what about *Peacekeeper*?"

"Because sometimes the dead can't walk anywhere. Law and order help keep the peace," Jay said slowly as she mulled it over. "I'll always think of her as *The Walking Dead*, but *Peacekeeper* can be her public name."

"Her?" Red raised one eyebrow.

"You're outnumbered, big guy," Rivka said.

"How so? Me, Chaz, Hamlet, Ankh, and Erasmus. That's five to three. I think the Peacekeeper is a 'him.'"

Lindy shook her head. "Let me get my stuff." She took a step toward the berthing.

"Wait," Red grumbled.

"Men are so easy," Lindy murmured.

"As a professional, I've lived by the code to choose my battles wisely. No good can come from fighting this one. It would be what is called 'a Pyrrhic victory.' I concede to her."

"I'll look up Pyrrhic after you two are on the ground." Lindy sat down next to Ankh. His eyes remained unfocused as he hugged the bundle that was Erasmus to his chest.

"The facility is located next to the interstellar communication array," Ankh said softly. The ship banked toward its designated target.

"Planetary control is furious with our flight path and failure to respond to their calls," Chaz reported calmly. "I shall continue to ignore them."

"Good call, Chaz," Rivka agreed. Red stood near the hatch, with the Magistrate behind him. They both wore their game faces. "Once more unto the breach, my friend. May we return to the *Peacekeeper* alive and well."

"Or die trying," Red added. "Amen, Magistrate."

"You are such a lunkhead. Thanks for taking those rounds meant for me on S'Korr."

"Let's not do that again," Red replied.

"We'll do our best, but *damn*, Red! I can't believe how badly things spiraled out of control."

"If you didn't do anything that mattered, the bad guys wouldn't be trying to kill you. People who fight for others make enemies, and people who challenge the mighty... Well, that's a whole different kind of enemy; ones who can hire armies. Time is not your friend, Magistrate."

"Quick in-and-out." Rivka looked at the ceiling. "Who am I meeting with, Chaz?"

"The facility manager, a Miss Lauton."

"Does she have any authority? Or bodyguards?" Rivka shrugged at the look Red gave her.

"She is the manager of the facility," Chaz replied evenly. Rivka rolled her eyes and shook her head.

"Zombie," Red said.

"Yup, going to have to do it the up-close-and-personal way. Just in case, here—take a couple of these." Rivka handed him two of Ankh's coins. Red dug under his armor to put one in his jeans pocket, and the other he put in a vest pouch. "It's going to be hard to convince them that we're all about the peace."

The ship touched down with a gentle bump. "The facility is directly before us," Chaz reported. Red slapped the big red button that they had put on the pad to open and close the hatch. The top opened to reveal a murky orange sky. The steps rotated into position based on the angle and how far the door had to go to reach the ground.

Red hurried down before giving the signal to Rivka. She followed him down, and they turned left. A building was labeled in the local language, which was instantly translated by their chips into Galactic Standard. Astrocom Support.

Red walked quickly toward the main doors, checking the rooftop for any movement. "I like your plan where you don't tell anyone you're coming or who you're going to meet. I like that a lot. Reduces the chances of getting ambushed. And with the *Peacekeeper*'s guns trained on everything nearby, I think maybe the name fits *her* quite nicely," Red said over his shoulder while his eyes darted left to right and up to down in his never-ending search for threats.

"We can't be caught watching the paint dry. What the hell do I do for a vacation, Red? Is becoming a Magistrate a life sentence?"

"I'm not the one to answer that. I'll do everything in my power to make sure you don't die on my watch. Two months into this gig, and we've gotten close, what…twenty, thirty times?"

"You're funny, Red. I think I'll judge you last."

"I like the new food dispenser. Who would have known it was the freaking programming that was making the food taste like shit?"

"But you were eating it!"

"I was hungry," Red replied. He hurried to the door, looking through the glass before opening it. "I need X-ray eyeballs."

"I'll check with the Pod-doc and see if we can get you some of those."

"Be sharp, Magistrate. This could be the lion's den." Red whipped the door open and rushed through, stopping two steps inside so Rivka could follow.

No one was there. An unadorned staircase led upward from the main doorway. One door-lined hallway went to the left, and one to the right.

"That was anti-climactic," Rivka said. "Is that an office roster?"

Red looked where she pointed. "Looks like it." He watched as she looked for the manager's office.

"Lauton. She's on the second floor." Red went up the

stairs first, climbing quickly. Rivka trailed behind. He reached the landing and looked left then right at a mirror of the first floor. He shook his head. Rivka went right, and after two rooms, determined that the office was on the other side. Two females entered the left hallway from an office, screamed at the sight of the Magistrate's bodyguard, and ran back inside, slamming the door behind them.

"What'd you do?" Rivka snickered. "Next time, try smiling."

"That'll work. They won't notice the hardware. Maybe it was the grenades that put them on edge."

"I'm sure that was it. You better let me go first. I don't think we want them to have heart failure when your big ass darkens their doorway." Rivka brushed her hair from her face and opened the door to the office with the plate that unsurprisingly read, Miss Lauton, Facility Manager.

Rivka put on her biggest smile and strolled in, complete with ballistic vest and leggings, her Magistrate's jacket open. "Miss Lauton?" she asked.

The female at the only desk in the room shook her head. "She was fired yesterday."

Rivka's smile turned into a deep frown. "Do you know why?"

"I'm sorry. Even if I did, I wouldn't tell a stranger."

"My apologies. I'm Magistrate Rivka Anoa, and I'm here on behalf of the Federation to examine some irregularities being broadcast through your computers."

The female recoiled in shock; not from the question, but at Red when he leaned into the room. "I don't have any money!" she cried out.

"I'll need you to calm down."

Rivka pulled out her datapad. A message was waiting.

Not yet.

"We need to see your systems," Rivka informed her through a beaming smile.

"I'm going to have to verify this," the female said.

"With whom?" Rivka wondered. "I suspect you're the temporary facility manager?"

"Yes." She tapped on her old-style keyboard. Rivka tapped on her screen.

How is this backward planet the lead in an intergalactic cybercrime?

The system we're looking for is buried beneath the veneer of old technology. Find the main systems. Probably in the basement.

"We'd like to go to the basement now, and you're going to escort us."

"I'm sorry, but I can't do that," the female said, suddenly growing a spine.

"Thanks for calling Security." Rivka walked around the desk. "Where are the servers?"

She pulled the female to her feet, seeing the door to the basement in her mind. She also saw the warning flashing on the computer screen. "Illegal Planetary Landing. Security forces are on their way."

"Red, Security is on their way. Go to the basement and give Ankh access. I'll stay here to find where Miss Lauton lives. I don't believe in coincidences."

"I can't leave you alone."

"I need access to those computers, and I need you back here before your presence is necessary. Now go! Take a left at the stairs. Basement door is the last on the left." Rivka yelled. Red gritted his teeth for a moment before pounding down the hall.

"Give me Lauton's address."

"No," the female refused firmly, risking a glance out the window to where the spaceship was filling the roadway. "What the heck?"

"Your boys are going to have a tough time getting past my ride."

"Boys?"

"You know. Security."

"There are no boys here. There are only females on this planet."

"That's interesting and something we'll talk about later, but right now I need you to show me the records on the facility manager."

"No." The female crossed her arms. Rivka pushed the female back into the chair, holding onto her wrist as she did so.

"What's your password?"

"What?"

Rivka typed it in with one finger.

"How did you do that?"

"I pushed down on the keys and it showed on the screen," Rivka replied flippantly. The female attempted to reach the keyboard, but Rivka threw her back so hard that the chair flipped over. "You're starting to piss me off."

"They said you were coming. An impostor trying to get into our systems. I won't let you!"

"And Miss Lauton would have, I suspect. That was why she had to go. She wasn't complicit in all this. There's hope for your planet, whatever your name is. The easy answer for me is to kill you, or you could sit there quietly and wait for me to finish."

Rivka flipped through the various systems. The going was slow since she didn't know the Zaxxon logic. "I need your help," she conceded, grabbing the female's wrist again. "Where are the files?"

Two clicks later the personnel data appeared. Lauton's address was there. Rivka made sure the datapad recorded it, then kicked the monitor to crack the screen and tossed the computer out the window. "I can't leave you here to tell tales, so you're coming with me.

A sharp retort told her that the *Peacekeeper* was engaging someone. "Sounds like Security has arrived. I doubt they brought an army, but now would be a good time for us to leave. Come on."

The *thud* of a heavy stride and jingle of weaponry announced Red's return. Rivka stepped into the hall, dragging the recalcitrant female with her.

"You're going to have to kill her," Red stated matter-of-factly and leveled his railgun. She fainted dead away. "Will she stay out for as long as we need?"

"I hope so, because I'm tired of dragging her dumb ass and it's only been ten meters."

Red turned on his heel and ran back down the hall. "Get into your office!" he yelled at someone Rivka couldn't see. They descended the steps three at a time, hit the bottom at a dead run, banged the door open, and sprinted to the ship. In the distance, lights flashed from emergency vehicles.

Once inside, Red slammed the door button with the palm of his big hand. "Chaz, take us to the address I gave you. Next stop, Miss Lauton's home."

15

"We will be there in thirty seconds," Chaz announced. Rivka was in the short hall to the bridge, but turned around and headed back to where Red waited by the hatch.

"Ankh, tell me you got in."

Jay answered. "They got in. Ankh said something about taking a victory lap before he disappeared back into his crazy communion with his AI."

"Has Ankh ever run a step in his life? He doesn't strike me as the physical sort," Red muttered.

"He got in." Rivka smiled. "And he found what we needed him to find. I hope we don't have to hit those other five planets. I'm tired of the running and gunning. I'm a lawyer, for Pete's sake. I know people are usually pissed at us, but generally, it's not on a global scale."

"We have a nice spaceship," Red offered.

"There is that," Rivka replied.

The spaceship touched down. There was a metallic

crunch from underneath. "Straight out the hatch, Magistrate," Chaz directed.

Red mashed the button and hit the steps at a dead run because speed was his friend. Rivka raced after him. There was one house in a small wooded area, squarish and desert tan. Red peeled off and let Rivka continue to the door. He faced the spaceship and watched the open areas on either side of it.

Rivka studied the door before pounding on it. There was a button next to the door with a screen above. She pushed it.

After receiving no response, she pushed it again. Rivka raised her hand to pound on the door when a face appeared on the small screen.

"Go away!"

Rivka looked at the harried female in the image and instantly felt sorry for her. "I am Magistrate Rivka Anoa, here on behalf of the Federation. I think you might have information that can help me in an ongoing investigation into the companies that have been doing business with your old employer. I believe your firing was to impede my efforts."

The door opened. Lauton looked even more frazzled in person.

"We know about the fake money going through your systems. We also know that you didn't direct it," Rivka stated, watching for the body language to tell her if she had hit the mark. Lauton fell forward into Rivka's arms.

Exhaustion from not sleeping, dehydration from not drinking, weak from lack of food. She'd been under pressure since the beginning of Rivka's investigation. In her mind flashed angry conversations when she had discovered that the vast majority of transactions were fabricated by computers she never knew existed that were tied into their main system. Her demise had been imminent once she'd refused to play.

"I suspect your life is in jeopardy. You need to come with me if you want to live."

"We got company, Magistrate!" Red shouted. The *Peacekeeper's* weapons started to fire, creating a barrier through which the security mob couldn't pass. "Time to go!"

Rivka hoisted the female onto her shoulder. "You'll thank me later." She started to run with Red at her side as they raced for the steps into the ship. A head appeared where one shouldn't have been, and Red fired his railgun. The hypersonic dart tore into the ground, spraying a cloud of dirt into the prying eyes.

"I love my gun!" Red declared.

"Why are we always running?" Rivka asked between breaths as she bounded up the steps, the female over her shoulder not slowing her down. "I hate running."

Once inside, Red mashed the button, retracting the stairs and securing the hatch. "Get us out of here!" Rivka ordered. She plopped Lauton into a seat.

The ship lifted off and angled sharply upward as it headed for the stars. "Gravitic shields are up," Chaz reported.

"Are they going to try and stop us from leaving?" Rivka asked.

"Sensors show some movement from ships in orbit around the planet, but nothing suggesting an attempt to interfere with our departure."

"Then why the shields?"

"Because we don't trust anyone," the evolving EI replied.

"I like the way you think, Chaz. The farther we get into this Mandolin cesspool, the worst things stink. I stopped looking for predicate crimes a long time ago. We have the thread and are pulling it. The racket is starting to unravel."

"This seems more like a war than a legal action, Magistrate. Excuse me for being forward." Red sounded contrite. "Don't get me wrong, I like blowing shit up as much as the next guy, and this railgun is the cat's ass—no disrespect, Hamlet—but I can't protect you if all we're doing is fighting. I'm supposed to be the guy in the background, invisible because all eyes are on what you're doing. But they aren't. We're side by side, fighting our way through a determined enemy who seems to have unlimited resources. We have *Peacekeeper* and us. That's it."

Red waved his arm to take in the group packed into the recreation room—a Crenellian with his AI, a Zaxxon, four humans, and a cat.

Rivka sat forward with her elbows on her knees and her head in her hands. "It's not supposed to be like this. The vast majority of Federation citizens are law abiding. They want to live their lives free from interference, doing the daily grind for their families. I believe that. If we toppled Mandolin tomorrow, most people on these planets wouldn't know the difference. Bad Company would step back in and start filling orders. Bulk freighters would arrive, possibly from the same places as before, carrying the same supplies but showing a different flag."

Jay offered Lauton a glass of water and a spaghetti and meatballs bar, the crew's new favorite meal.

Lindy helped Red remove his gear. "No new holes?"

He laughed and shook his head. "Only the ones I was born with."

She groaned, and Jay feigned gagging.

"I'm looking into Mandolin Partnership and their interference with business affairs. Zaxxon Major is one of more than twenty planets who have become slaves to Mandolin," Rivka started to explain.

Lauton shrugged. "I've never heard of Mandolin. We deal with Gargeath for our interstellar shipments of goods, and Lameeris for the digital billing, which is the most lucrative enterprise on Zaxxon Major!" Lauton spoke proudly, but the looks on the others' faces dampened her enthusiasm. "That was last week, before I knew all of it was a sham."

The wind gone from her sails; she once again looked sick and frail. Lauton was human in appearance, except for her lack of ears, which were covered by a shock of bright red hair. Her eyes were a vivid blue. Lauton leaned back in the chair and studied the faces that looked at her.

"What now?" she asked, barely above a whisper. "Zaxxon Major is my home."

"And you'll return to it when it's safe. For now, I'm taking you into protective custody. Hang out on the ship while we do our thing. Ankh? What did you learn from tapping the gold mine? Ankh?"

They waited until he blinked and focused on the Magistrate. "Yes?"

"What did you find out, and what next?" Rivka asked again.

"Didn't you read the report?" Ankh shot back in an even tone.

"What report?" Rivka mouthed before pulling her datapad from her pocket and opening the flashing icon where the new report was waiting. She zeroed in on the words and inhaled the text, harking back to her law school days where she had devoured mountains of information to generate single consolidated reports supported by legal positions both pro and con, never knowing which side she'd be picked to present.

Rivka ran a finger along a flash burn across the front of her coat. "I miss law school," she inadvertently said aloud.

"I thought it was only me," Jay replied.

"You've never been to law school." Rivka looked confused.

"I'm joking, because you look like you're going to cry."

"No, not going to cry. I worked so hard to study the law, yet here I am on the enforcement end getting shot at."

"You're getting shot at because you are making a case for how people are breaking the law. There is a war, but it's between the criminals and the law-abiding," Jay clarified.

"I'm on the outside looking in," Lindy started. "What I see is a lot of effort on your part to get to the people behind the crime and doing what you can to keep from harming those caught in the middle, even if they broke the law. Had it not been for Oscura Mandel, they would still be walking the straight and narrow."

"Keeping the peace," Red added softly, "by stopping one crime at a time."

Rivka stood and locked her hands behind her back. "We are seeing people's true natures, as revealed by the extremes of wealth and poverty. Each strips the veneer away, making what is underneath visible. We've seen the worst of civilization, and we'll continue to see the worst the galaxy has to offer because those are the people we have to stop. Someone has to stand between the power brokers like Oscura Mandel, or 'Nefas,' as he is called, and people like Lauton, innocents only trying to do their job."

Rivka paced back and forth. The space only allowed three steps before she had to turn around.

"Where should we go?" Chaz interrupted.

"We need to set up for a final assault. Because of the lucrative nature of what we found hidden beneath the servers on Zaxxon Prime, we only need to explore two other planets before going to Morinvaille," Erasmus explained.

"I'm not looking forward to that," Rivka said, stopping to look at Ankh.

"Where do you wish us to go now?" Chaz pressed.

"Take us to these coordinates in the Corrhen Cluster," Erasmus replied. "Ankh and I have analyzed the situation. Mandel has known where we were going because we did not hide our movements. The Magistrate arranged meetings well ahead of time; meetings with people who were later determined to be in Mandel's pocket. With current hostilities bordering on open warfare, the Magistrate no longer has the pleasure of announcing her schedule. We will go to the Corrhen Cluster, where we will establish meeting requests with every major player on every planet in question, including those we've already visited."

A Gate formed as soon as *Peacekeeper* cleared the upper atmosphere. It slipped over the event horizon and was gone from Zaxxon space.

The ship remained motionless in the shadow of a dead moon orbiting an inhospitable planet of an uninhabited system in the Corrhen Cluster. Erasmus and Chaz were coordinating the barrage of requests for meetings to happen simultaneously across fifty light-years of space and multiple planets.

Rivka was only going to make one of them. Quarst was a small planet, but it had one hundred and twenty-four moons and a polar cap that was necessary to cool the power plants for the most energy-dependent race in the galaxy. The entirety of the planet's small livable area had been developed by the Quarries, a race of quadrupeds. Humans called them 'Centaurs,' but the Quarries didn't see the resemblance.

They liked their machines and comforts. What better place to set up a money-laundering operation?

"The Quarst president has a great deal to answer for," Erasmus told them. "I have picked it as one of the final two worlds because it has seen the greatest upheaval since contracting with one of Mandolin's sub-sub-subcontractors. The planet has suffered under the president's leadership, and there is no end in sight. I believe that he will be the most malleable under interrogation."

Rivka chewed on the inside of her lip. "Let me see your analysis." Almost instantly, the report appeared on her datapad. She sat down to read it. Red excused himself to clean his gear and put it away. Lindy went with him. Jay started talking with Lauton about life on Zaxxon Major.

After a while, Lauton's lip started to tremble and tears welled in her eyes. "Will I get to see my home again?"

Rivka looked up from her pad. "Not only yes, but *hell* yes. Once we dismantle the racketeering operation, Zaxxon will need people like you more than ever. You built up an operation without knowing about the billing and payments that were cycling through. What if you could integrate the secret systems with the ones you already have to jump Zaxxon up the technological scale? They will need people like you when the corrupt are out of power. We'll take you back when it's safe."

Lauton nodded and became lost in her own thoughts.

"Erasmus, you said that Quarst and Belheeake should give us what we need," Rivka mused.

"From the systems on Zaxxon Major, I was able to find the links to the shell companies. There are thousands of them. I've established a database for lookup purposes. It will give you the links from any company back to Mandolin. I'll project the final links on the big screen."

The recreation room's main screen lit up, and Mandolin Partnership appeared at the top. The next level showed a dozen companies, and the next showed numbers instead of names. The third level had more than a hundred shell companies. The majority of the money laundering took place between the third and fourth levels.

"From the fourth level to the sixth a great deal of work takes place, so I don't categorize them as shell companies. Rather, they are real companies with an operations element that is outside Federation control. They still have to manage the supply chain, but they also have to integrate the smuggling part of the business, which is a secondary supply chain. It's a great deal of work, done by both computers and living beings. People are employed in these businesses and have families that they are taking care of. Most probably don't know they are part of a corrupt operation." Erasmus paused.

"When Mandel is toppled, what happens to them?"

"If Bad Company needs their services, they'll continue. If not, they'll be out of a job."

"How many of these people were employed in this sector before?"

"Fewer than are employed now," Erasmus replied. "About fifty percent fewer."

"The law giveth and the law taketh away." Rivka scowled. "Not all victims look the same, and some don't even know they are victims."

"What can we do about it?" Jay asked while getting Lauton more water and another food bar.

"I'd like to say I know, but I don't. I'll call Grainger, or maybe Nathan Lowell. This is bigger than just me." Rivka thought about what she'd said. "You know, I can't call Nathan. By judging Mandel as a racketeer and Mandolin as a corrupt organization, I hand all the contracts back to the Bad Company, of which Nathan is the president. I can't give the impression that he took out a competitor by sending the law after them. Maybe I'll investigate the Bad Company after this."

"The hand that feeds you?" Jay asked.

"No one is above the law," Rivka recited. "Although, I

have had dealings with the Bad Company in the past, and am comfortable that they are complying. There we go. Investigation complete, but I still can't tell Nathan about the progress of this one."

"But if there is a void following the downfall of Mandolin—and I know you're going to kick their asses right up around their ears—wouldn't Nathan need to be ready to jump in?"

"What if he shows his hand before we're ready to drop the hammer?"

"You need to talk to him and tell him your concerns. How many people are going to be hurt, besides that Mandel guy and his partner?"

"Too many, I expect. I love the law," Rivka reiterated. "My compliance with it in pursuit of this case has, however, become problematic. I'll be on the bridge. I have a couple of people I need to talk with."

Rivka secured the hatch behind her because she didn't want any underwear-clad people showing up in the background while she was trying to carry on serious conversations. "Contact Grainger," she requested.

The main screen appeared with a large dark box that slowly illuminated to show Grainger's face, complete with pillow lines and hair standing up.

"No way!" he mumbled. "Zombie calling me in the middle of the night. How strange is that?"

"Everywhere we go, people are shooting at us. The ship was attacked in space. This is more like a war than a legal action. What the hell?" she told him without preamble.

"I saw your interim reports. I also saw data provided by

your computer genius, who stated unequivocally that your ship was in no real danger."

"He clearly has more confidence in his AI than I have in the ineptitude of our enemy. I'm collecting evidence, but at this point, it's more to make sure that we completely dismantle the racket. Mandolin committed the crime of bribery, until it became attempted murder. He has no inhibitions out here. I am the first to challenge him. Why haven't the Federation's armed forces dealt with this guy?"

Grainger scratched his head and yawned. "The Federation uses the Bad Company's Direct Action Branch, a small mercenary group that you've already met. The Federation also has a great number of single-ship teams carrying out intelligence collection and small-unit missions. And then there is the Force de Guerre, a more traditional invasion and occupation force, but they are already engaged. The rest of the Federation armed forces, as we'll call them, are provided by member planets. Is it any surprise that the planets Mandolin picked do not have militaries? I would love to request a tactical team to support you, but there isn't one. The *War Axe* isn't available either, because of the unidentified destroyer that's harassing Keeg Station."

"Are they okay? It looked like a real shitstorm when we stopped by to pick up Ankh and Erasmus."

"They're doing what they do—fighting like banshees— but despite the appearance of one hundred against one, it is an even match. You'll get your support as soon as possible, hopefully before you have to go to Morinvaille."

"'Hopefully?'"

"The longer this case drags out, the harder it will be to pin down the perps. Those scumbags have made enough that they can buy a new planet and start over. You need to collect the evidence so Ankh can help the Federation's best accountants set up triggers to identify something like this before it grows beyond a single planet."

"But why did they send a lawyer when a bunch of forensic accountants, computer whizzes, and a combat unit could have accomplished the same thing and done it without risk to life or limb?"

"Now you know why most of the Magistrates were warriors, soldiers, or hell-raisers before earning the pin. You were the first one who came to us as a legal eagle, but once you showed your gift and took the law into your own hands, you became one of us. That's why you're in the middle of the storm, Magistrate. You ever hear the phrase 'sink or swim?'"

"I hate that expression."

"Maybe so, but this is your time to swim."

16

"This is my time to swim," Rivka repeated after the communication channel had closed. She left the bridge to join those in the rec room. Lauton was asleep, and Jay had her headphones on so she could watch a movie without bothering anyone else.

Ankh was embroiled in a private conversation with his AI. Rivka could tell by the way he gripped the pack containing Erasmus and his face, which was locked in a thousand-meter stare. Red and Lindy were in the back somewhere.

She poked the Crenellian's shoulder and he nearly jumped out of his skin, but he didn't lose his grip on the pack. "Don't do that," he said evenly when his breathing calmed. "What?'

"Can you sever the links between Morinvaille and the two planets where you think we'll find all that damning evidence?"

"Why would I need to cut the links if we're going to Morinvaille last?"

"What if we go there first, cut the heads off the hydra, and then not have people trying to kill us when we show up?"

"But our analysis was definitive in that we need to go Quarst and Belheeake first."

"As soon as we show up, someone tips off Mandel and he sics the dogs on us. If there is no Mandel, there will be no dogs. The last thing he expects is for us to knock on his front door."

"He won't let you in. His empire will continue its operations because you'll be neutralized."

"Then Grainger will come after him. The Magistrates will keep coming until Justice is served."

Ankh considered what she had said before replying, "Of course we can cut Mandolin off from everything outside their home planet, but can we do it before they transmit a signal to destroy the evidence or summon reinforcements? That's the question."

"I have full confidence in you, Ankh. Do I have an appointment scheduled with Oscura Mandel, Chairman, President, and CEO of Mandolin Partnership?"

Ankh communed briefly with Erasmus. "Your appointment is confirmed, Magistrate."

"How close can you Gate us to our landing coordinates?"

"Erasmus can put *Peacekeeper* millimeters from reentry. We'll exit the Gate into the turbulence of the upper atmosphere."

"That's as close as you can get?"

Ankh stared at her without answering.

"I'll take that as a yes. I never studied astromechanics,

so I don't know. That's why we ask questions, Ankh—to learn."

"You are supposed to go to Morinvaille last." Ankh held her gaze as she slowly shook her head.

"Change of plans, my friend. It's time to swim with the big dogs. I have enough evidence to put him away, so I don't need any more. Ordering the destruction of our ship was a capital crime. It's also something I take personally, so we can stop fucking around with the preliminaries. It's time to go for the throat. I need you to cut all signals from the planet and keep those communications systems offline until I give the all-clear."

"I will need the configuration of any space-based communication relays to improve our chances."

"No can do. If we start snooping around, they'll destroy everything and disappear. When we show up, I expect all hell to break loose."

"If they destroyed everything and disappeared, doesn't that achieve your goal?"

"Everything except for Justice. They have a great deal to answer for."

"None of the planets they operate on are showing any problems," Ankh replied.

"That isn't an argument. On the face of it, most RICO crimes seem to be victimless, but they aren't. People lose their free will, becoming slaves to a system they can't change. There are lots of victims, but they have put on brave faces. Lauton is a victim. Does she look okay?"

The Zaxxon was sleeping comfortably, but her features were drawn. Even with her eyes closed, the dark circles were prominent.

Ankh's expression didn't change.

"If you don't have the time for a digital separation, maybe we can do something a little more hands-on."

"Boarding a comm relay satellite is ill-advised at the best of times," Ankh retorted.

"How about if we just blow it up?"

"What if there is more than one?"

"Then you have responsibility for the others. Will there be more than one? Morinvaille is a tiny planet with a small habitable area."

"It's also outside Federation borders."

"But by doing business within the Federation, they come under our jurisdiction. They still answer to us. They came into our house and broke our laws. It's time to pay the piper. I'm going to get a couple hours of sleep. Once we start sliding down this mountain, there'll be no stopping until we reach the bottom."

"We're in space. There is no mountain," Ankh told Rivka, who was already on her way to her cabin.

"*Hamlet!*" she grumbled when she saw the hairball on her pillow.

"Chaz, connect me to Terry Henry Walton, please." Rivka sat watching the main screen.

The bridge was quiet. Red stood behind the captain's chair, fully outfitted in his gear. He carried the shotgun in a case over his shoulder and the railgun in his arms. The vest's pouches were filled with grenades. Rivka had him on display to convince TH that they needed his help.

"Barrister, not a good time," Colonel Walton answered. The image bounced before settling.

"We're going to confront Mandolin Partnership directly. Since they've tried to kill us every step of the way, we're skipping everything else and going straight for the jugular. We are going to be outgunned. I was hoping you'd be able to join us, but I see that your situation may be as bad as mine."

"We're trying not to destroy this guy because we want the technology that he used as he toyed with us, but I've had about enough of this bastard. Ted can try to reverse-engineer it from the billions of pieces floating through space. Kill that ship!" Terry shouted at someone offscreen. "Dammit."

"If you can make it or send anyone else, we'd appreciate it. I'm transmitting the coordinates to you. If you don't hear from us, that's where the next expedition needs to go."

"You're better than they are," Terry said.

"How do you know?"

"Because if you go in there thinking anything different, you've already lost. No fight is easy until it's over. Gotta run. Get my suit ready!" Terry's screen went dark as he ran after his words. The *War Axe* was getting hammered. Even if they destroyed the enemy, would they be in any shape to help the Magistrate enforce the law?

"If we die," Red started slowly, "it'll be inside the atmosphere. Our fireball will be glorious."

"Is that empathy, or your idea of a motivational speech? Today is a great day to die!"

"No, it isn't."

"But that's... Never mind." Rivka shook her head as she

continued to look at the blank screen. "Chaz, I need you and Erasmus to coordinate your efforts. Destroy the space-based array, which I assume they have because they must. And then we're going to the planet's surface. We need some kind of leverage so that Mandel is forced to meet with me."

"Lie," Red suggested.

"Explain."

"Tell him that you are holding the evidence in a safe place, to be transmitted in case anything happens to you."

"I like it. Why would that be a lie?"

"Are you stoned? Send the evidence now! You've made your case. All you have to do is tie the bow on the package. My job is to keep you alive. On a personal note, you are stretching the limits of me being able to do my job."

"You have a point, Red. You don't have to go with me to see Oscura Nefas Mandel. This is my responsibility. I don't want your death on my shoulders."

"What the fuck is wrong with you?" Red demanded, pounding on the back of the chair with a massive fist. He held his railgun up, which emphasized his angry scowl.

"What do you mean by that?" Rivka glowered back.

"Besides it being my job, do you think you haven't earned my loyalty? You know that I'm a wanted man— wanted because I wouldn't take a bullet for my last two scumbag employers. I broke their contracts. They were criminals, and although I could turn a blind eye to some of their dealings, I wouldn't let them buy my soul. I would take a bullet for you, Rivka, because you've earned it, not because Grainger would kick my ass or I wouldn't get paid. I swear that I will keep you alive or die trying. And now that I have a girlfriend, I'd like to avoid that 'die trying' part."

"I didn't know you were wanted, but I suspect Grainger does." Red nodded. "Thanks. For the record, I'm not a big fan of the dying part either. Let's try your leverage while seeing how Ankh and Erasmus can spoof Mandel and his cronies into thinking that they need more time."

"What's your plan, Magistrate? Are you going to execute them on sight?" Red asked.

"I need to touch them while they're still alive, just to make sure we find what they're hiding. This is a hydra. Seven heads that we need to cut off, and if we don't get them at the same time, they'll grow back, bigger and badder than before."

"If you need me to blow shit up, I'd like to see what the railgun can do on full auto if there's an opportunity."

"Before the day is out, I think we'll be tired of all the opportunities we're going to have."

"I'm not sure how I should feel about that, besides hungry. I'd suggest we take a picnic lunch, but that space in my pack is reserved for extra ammo. I can miss a meal, but not a reload." Red left the bridge and turned into the rec room. "Ankh, what other food programs did you install? I've had my fill of spaghetti bars for a while."

Wearing his usual blank expression, Ankh faced Red. "You people eat enough to feed an entire Crenellian city."

Red smiled. "I feel pride swelling in my breast."

Rivka shrugged, a half-smile on her face. "We burn a lot of calories. I think it's the running."

"So, you think I'm your girlfriend, do you?" Lindy questioned. She leaned against the wall of the corridor to the berthing area, her arms crossed. Lauton remained behind her, watching with interest as she'd had almost no dealings with males.

"You're *my* girlfriend," Jay offered as she walked past.

"You got that right, girlfriend," Lindy shot back.

Red turned to Rivka, his face pleading. "I don't know what's going on."

Rivka started to laugh before biting her lip. Lindy winked.

"I guess I can give my notice, but you know what that means."

Red was all smiles once again. "That you're my girlfriend?"

"That's just a name, you big goon. It means you won't get special treatment at the AGB restaurant."

"Oh." Red dragged the word out. He looked at Rivka and mouthed the word, 'Girlfriend.' Rivka nodded, and Red was all smiles again.

"I swear," Rivka said, "men are such babies."

"Hey!"

"You outnumber us, remember? You, Hamlet, Chaz, Ankh, and Erasmus. That's a Crenellian, a cat, and two AIs. All that *testosterone* is wearing us poor girls down."

Ankh pointed to the food processor as a bar popped into the tray. Red took a tentative bite. "Peanut butter and jelly!" he exclaimed. Lindy still had her arms crossed. Red swallowed before continuing. "I find myself in a strange position where no matter how much weaponry I have, I am in a battle that I cannot win. I defer and surrender." He bowed until his head was even with the table. He stood up and took another big bite, talking to the dispenser as he chewed. "Three more of those, please."

"I don't know why you see it as a battle when it's more of a partnership. Don't you think, girlfriend?" Lindy asked.

"I do think that, girlfriend."

Red started to look uncomfortable again. Lindy cornered him in the galley. She tried to wrap her arms around his neck, but with his combat gear on she couldn't get close enough. She pulled his face down to hers. "You may be a big goon, but you're *my* big goon. Don't you dare die on me." She kissed him in a way that promised much more.

As long as he returned to the ship when it was over.

"Magistrate?" he wondered.

"Yeah. It's about that time, isn't it?" Rivka got Ankh's attention.

"Yes, yes. We will Gate in exactly two minutes and twelve seconds. It could be a very rough ride, and everything will happen quickly between our arrival and touchdown. You should strap yourselves in," Ankh recommended.

The crew took their seats and tightened their belts. Lauton took an empty seat and did as the others did. Hamlet appeared and jumped into Jay's lap. She wrapped protective arms around the cat. Red's lip twitched.

"We won't get a cat," Lindy stated.

"Or a dog," Red added.

"I did like the wombat, though. She was big and soft and cuddly, like someone else I know."

"You can't mean me. I'm not sure I've ever been called soft."

"One minute," Erasmus announced.

Rivka buckled into the captain's chair on the bridge. "Bring up the view outside the ship. All angles, please. Put the tactical situation on the left screen."

The main screen showed the vast emptiness of space. The right side view showed the darkness of a dead moon wearing the aura of the sun that shone behind it. The left side showed the planet, a moon, and *Peacekeeper*. No other objects warranted space on the screen.

"Ten seconds," Erasmus reported and started the countdown. Rivka's muscles tightened, even though she knew going through the Gate would be painless. The main screen showed the circle of light that appeared when the Gate engine activated. The main engines engaged to drive the ship through at a higher rate of speed than normal.

Peacekeeper emerged on the other side, firing before clearing the event horizon. The systems continued firing even after a satellite in the distance came apart. The ship targeted the biggest pieces, blowing them to near-vapor. The ship dove radically and started to heat up with reentry. The flames of friction shrouded the shields, making the corvette a massive fireball in a steep descent toward the planet's surface.

The ship was buffeted, and it jerked as it reacted to the turbulence outside. When the corvette's flight smoothed, Rivka unbuckled and headed for the exit. Red was one step behind her, having had to come from the rec room. He pushed past to be in front of the door, per their standard operating procedure.

They were making it up as they went.

"Chaz, what does tactical show? How many ships in orbit?"

"None, Magistrate. The planet appears to have been abandoned."

"Say what?" Rivka was outraged. Her ploy had failed.

"Instructions?" Red asked.

"Stay the course. I need to see for myself." Rivka clenched her jaw and growled. "No ships on the surface either?"

"There is one ship, Magistrate."

"Operational?"

"Yes."

"That means there is someone we can talk to." A smile crept slowly across her face. It wasn't a pleasant look. Red was happy not to be on the receiving end of what she had in mind for whoever they came across.

"Abandoned. A ploy, maybe?" Red suggested.

"If we treat it as hostile and well-populated, we'll be no worse for the wear. The alternative could get us killed."

"My thoughts exactly."

With a final maneuver, the ship settled to the ground.

"Ready?" the big man asked.

"I expect we'll be running?"

"You would be right."

"I hate running."

"Me, too." Red slapped the button, raised his railgun, and ran out while the stairs were still descending. He jumped to the ground and continued directly for the only building in the area. Rivka hurried to catch up. She didn't sense anyone or anything. It seemed that even with her unpredictability, they'd guessed her move.

She slowed when Red reached the front entrance and yanked the door open. He waved impatiently at her. She walked up the stairs to the building. He scanned the inside before tearing through the doorway and diving to the side.

"Clear," he reported. Rivka walked in like she owned the place. It looked more like a home than a workplace. She continued through the well-appointed entry, with its couches and chairs. There was a wet bar on one side and a fireplace on the other.

"What the hell is this?" Rivka asked.

Red kept his thoughts to himself. His eyes danced across the nooks and crannies of the great room, identifying the numerous exits and tagging them for movement. He couldn't shoot first since Rivka wanted live bodies to interrogate. But there was nothing alive.

"Hello?" Rivka ventured. It didn't echo because of wall hangings and soft cushions on the seats. "Interesting. What do you say we start at the top and work our way down?"

Red nodded and led the way up a wide curving stairway. The building was massive, but only two stories were aboveground. Red jogged down a long corridor with Rivka trotting after him. When he reached the end, he picked a door at random and checked to see if it was unlocked. The handle turned, and the door opened soundlessly into a bedroom with an attached bath, both empty.

"This place is giving me the creeps," Red grumbled.

"I thought it was just me," Rivka admitted. Despite Red's objections, they opened doors simultaneously on opposite sides of the corridor. Bedrooms, a workout room, a dining room, and when Rivka opened the door to a modern office, she yelled for Red. He sprinted to her as if she were under attack. She shrugged and threw the door open.

Red raised his railgun and entered, the barrel going where his eyes went. He swung the weapon viciously as he searched the room. Rivka sat at the first desk and tried to access the computer. Even with the power on, the system was dead. "I think they trashed their computers and bailed. We may have won the battle, but we haven't won the war."

"Something isn't right. Even if they had a week or two heads-up, they still couldn't have evacuated this place while also scrubbing it of any evidence. Watch the door," Red told her as he lifted the computer box to the desktop. He removed a small toolset from one of his pouches and started taking the case off. Inside was a dusty circuit board that may never have run a computer. "It's a fake."

"Which means a trap." Rivka ran out the door and skipped the other rooms lining the corridor on her way to the stairs. Red ran, but couldn't catch her.

17

R ivka hit the bottom floor, went to the first door she found, and opened it to find more of the same.

"It's all a facade," she said over her shoulder. Red waited in the doorway, breathing heavily and studying the room. Together, they checked the next room and the next. Rivka finally removed her datapad to contact the ship. "Do the ship's sensors show anything?" she asked.

Chaz replied, "Infrared shows that you are the only warm-blooded creatures in the aboveground portion of the structure."

"There are signatures below ground?"

"The sensors can't penetrate the barrier."

Rivka slapped her forehead. "Red, make sure that when we get home, we get the full military upgrade. The team needs to have instantaneous communication at all times."

"That doesn't sound like the lawyer I met not so long ago."

Rivka hung her head. "It would be nice if that lawyer

could do her thing, but with criminals double-glazing that shit, I'm not left with much of a choice."

"'Double-glazing?'" Red asked, never looking at Rivka as he watched for enemies to appear from everywhere and nowhere.

"Gloss over, blow off, ignore. You know, double-glaze, like my eyes after watching some of Jay's movies."

"I'd rather watch paint dry," Red admitted. "So there's a basement that's shielded. All of this is eyewash. Down there is the real operation, and without comm, they may be a little bit torqued."

"I think the way down is probably right there," Rivka pointed to a double door at the side of the staircase.

"Shall we try it?" Red asked. Rivka shook her head and pointed to Red's railgun.

"When you need it open on the first pull, you don't fuck around with doorknobs."

Red stepped to the side. "Fire in the hole," he said softly before spinning the railgun through its automatic setting. The hypervelocity darts screamed into a heavily armored interior wall, but the darts were made of denser material and sent a spray of molten metal in all directions. Red traced a line around the door and kept firing until a section of the wall fell in, revealing an opening.

He stopped firing. Rivka kept her neutron-pulse weapon trained on the opening. It was set at two. She didn't want to kill anyone until she interrogated them using her gift.

Red approached the opening, keeping his railgun at the ready. The steps led down. Rivka opened her pad. "Can you see down below now?"

"It's like looking through a straw. We don't see anything besides the hole you cut through the shield."

"The shield is nothing more than thick metal."

"That is enough to block the infrared sensors," Chaz replied. "But there is also some kind of electronic shielding."

"But the way down the stairs is open?"

"Yes."

"Smell like a trap?" Rivka asked, at Red's facial expression. He removed a grenade and waved it. "I would like to rescind my previous order regarding doing all we can to take them alive. Fuck these guys."

She walked to the opening, dialed her neutron pulse weapon to eleven, and activated it as she waved it back and forth. *"You have been judged!"* she yelled.

"What if there were innocents down there?" Red asked.

"If they are down there, they aren't innocent." She tipped her chin toward the grenade.

"Fire in the hole," he whispered, pulling the pin and tossing the weapon down the stairs. They heard it bounce four times before it exploded. While the explosion was still echoing in their heads, Red threw the second grenade with as much velocity as he could generate. The next explosion came from much deeper.

He rushed into the opening and headed down the stairs, once again looking over the barrel of his weapon while he descended. The steps were wide and would have been well lit if the blast hadn't destroyed numerous sconces along the walls. Red didn't care about aesthetics. His eyes were on the target at the bottom—a landing that looked like it led into the complex. There was a sealed door.

"Motherfuckers." Red took aim at the jamb and unleashed a torrent of hypersonic darts. Rivka barely got her hands over her ears in time. Red shook his head to clear the ringing while the nanocytes in his body went to work repairing the damage.

He eased down the last of the stairs, pulled a grenade, and kicked the door in.

"Wait!" came a feminine voice from the other side.

Red hesitated. He had already pulled the pin and was holding the grenade. "Come out with your hands up!" Rivka shouted. Red shook his head vigorously. He was too close to the door. Rivka was a few steps behind and above him. A face appeared immediately in front of the railgun.

"Dammit, lady! That's a great way to get yourself shot."

"Stop right there," Rivka ordered. "Where's Nefas?"

"Who?"

Rivka didn't see a weapon, so she lunged down the stairs and grabbed for the female's arm, but she slapped something on Red's railgun and disappeared through the door. He sent the weapon spinning through after her. It was keyed to handprints so no one could use it beside him and Rivka. He tossed the grenade after the railgun, making sure to spin it so no one could grab it and throw it back.

After it exploded Red rushed through the door, dodging to the side once through. Rivka leaned around the destroyed jamb, ready to fire her neutron-pulse weapon. She saw a movement and fired. The female screamed in agony, stood straight up, bucked twice, and flopped over a couch onto the floor.

"Come out, Nefas!" Rivka yelled. Red's shotgun belched smoke and fire. Rivka couldn't see what he'd fired at. She coughed before the air cleared. He fired again. "Stop that. I can't see."

"Movement at my twelve o'clock. That's your three o'clock."

"I'm a lawyer, for fuck's sake," Rivka complained. "Nefas! Get your ass out here. We need to have a conversation!"

"Cease fire!" someone yelled from inside.

"I can take him down," Red said softly.

"Wait," Rivka replied. She ducked into the room, a massive space set up as living quarters. Curtained alcoves surrounded the room, making it impossible to see what laid beyond. Through one of them, Oscura Mandel stepped, his hands raised and an easy smile parting his lips. Rivka was revolted. His partner had just been killed, and he didn't seem to care.

"How many more are here?" Red asked, signaling for the man to stop. He kept walking. "One more step and you lose a leg."

Red changed his aim point. Mandel stopped and stood relaxed. "Magistrate Rivka Anoa. Finally, I get to make your acquaintance."

"Since you've been following me throughout the galaxy, you know that I'm not screwing around. I have all the evidence I need to put you on Jhiordaan for the rest of your days."

"You and I both know that isn't going to happen," he remarked.

"Oscura Mandel, I am charging you with the bribery of the officials on S'Korr, Show Low, and Zaxxon Major. I am charging you with interference with an official investigation, I think there are seven counts of that, but we'll get a correct tally when we fill out the paperwork. Most egregious for your personal crimes is ordering the destruction of my ship while I was on it. That rises to the level of conspiracy and attempted murder, five counts. Almost all of those are considered predicate crimes under the RICO statute, Racketeer-Influenced and Corrupt Organizations. I can't think of a better description of the Mandolin Partnership. If you bring up the enterprise element of the statute, I refer you to the partnership. You and your now-dead wife were together to initiate the bribes. Enterprise. Predicate Crimes. RICO applies. Together, it's a capital crime. So you are correct. You will never see prison."

Rivka checked behind her. Her senses were tingling, and she didn't know why. "Kill him," Rivka ordered.

Red fired almost instantly, but Nefas was faster. He dodged the shotgun slug and dashed through an alcove. Rivka aimed her device at the space and pressed the trigger. She waved it back and forth to cover all the space. Red fired his shotgun. It shredded the curtain.

Rivka peeked inside. Nothing. "Dammit." She held Red back. "One trap to the next. We need to find the controls and shut this place down. Then the ship's sensors can find him and whatever else is down here."

Red watched as Rivka started her search. After ten minutes, she determined that the controls had to be in one of the alcoves, or a space beyond the alcoves. She started on the far right. Behind the first door was a corridor with five doors on each side.

"Shit," Red mumbled. "Let's get the fuck out of here. We can seal it off, and the military can come in and do a proper clearing. With the two of us, our asses are hanging out big time."

"I would love to see Justice come to this guy, but it's okay if it doesn't happen today." Rivka waved her pulse weapon at all the alcoves, starting from the far right and going to the far left, taking care to keep Red behind her. Once finished, she ran for the blown door. Red backed up until he was in the doorway. The area around the door was in bad shape because of the grenade.

Red saw his railgun on the floor by the female's body. His eyes darted around the room one last time before he ran forward, angled, grabbed the railgun without slowing, and continued out the door. His heart pounded as he hammered his way up the stairs. He stopped to throw a grenade through the door into the underground.

Rivka reached the top. The grenade exploded, and Red continued up the stairs. The Magistrate jogged out the front door and up the stairs into the ship. Red took one last look before following Rivka in and securing the hatch.

"Fuck," Rivka snarled. She headed down the short corridor, turned left past the bridge, and walked into the rec room. She froze, and Red almost ran into her.

"I have something you want, and you have something I want. I think we can make a deal, don't you, Magistrate?" Nefas said while holding a knife across Lindy's throat. Red was so angry he started to shake. He raised his railgun. "We all know you don't want to fire that thing in here."

R ivka pushed the barrel down, risking a look to see what Mandel's partner had put on it. Chewing gum. Not an explosive, or an acid, or anything destructive. She stood in front of the railgun and bluffed.

Oscura Mandel was not bluffing. His blade was only too real.

"Relax, Red. We have a guest on board. Our ship's name is *Peacekeeper*. Apropos, don't you think, Mister Mandel?"

"My friends call me Nefas. Won't you be my friend, Rivka?"

The Magistrate moved to the side, keeping her hands where Nefas could see. She sat down, crossing her legs and her arms and looking blankly at the head of the Mandolin Partnership.

"I try not to be friends with criminals. That might give me a bad name."

Jay and Ankh were unconscious on the floor. Lauton and Hamlet were nowhere to be seen. Red quivered in place; if looks could kill. Lindy looked more angry than scared, but Mandel held her in an iron-fisted grip.

"Like your murder of a man set free by a jury of his peers? Your history is there for all to see. One minute, you are condemned for your capital crime, and the next, you're sitting in judgment. I don't understand what happened to change your situation, but with your murder of my associates, I can only assume that you are a hitman for the Federation. An assassin."

He let that sink in. Rivka tried not to let it bother her, but his arrow had hit too close to home.

"I told you what you are charged with and found guilty of," Rivka said coldly.

"No innocent until proven guilty? No opportunity to face my accusers? Sounds like a totalitarian dictatorship."

Rivka didn't have to wait long before Nefas made his real demands.

"I need your ship," he said. "You'll have to stay here, of course, but you'll find my quarters quite comfortable. Well, the part you didn't blow up. I *am* curious about the weapon you used to kill my partner. I would very much like to see that."

"I don't think you understand how Federation ships work. They cannot be jacked. The intelligence that runs them won't respond and will self-destruct before they allow themselves to fall into an enemy's hands. Chaz, introduce yourself."

"Yes, Magistrate," the evolving EI agreed. "My name is Chaz, and I am Federation Corvette Seven Seven Four, called *Peacekeeper*. I help the crew fly the ship. You are not part of the crew and never will be."

"My. That's definitive. New plan. My friend here," he caressed Lindy's throat with the knife blade, "and the so-called Magistrate, you stay. Everyone else, get off my ship."

"Ain't happening, Dick," Red replied. "If you hurt her, I will tear you apart with my bare hands, and I'm not leaving as long as you are threatening her."

"A watchdog. So loyal," Nefas teased. "That wasn't a request. How would you live with yourself, knowing that you were the cause of this young lady's demise? Plus, you'll need to carry these two." He nudged Jay and Ankh with his toe before backing himself into a corner. He held all the trump cards.

"Go on, Red. Take them off the ship," Rivka ordered. The bodyguard glared at her. "Trust me."

Red groaned and blew out a long breath, his eyes pleading with Lindy. She nodded slightly. Red's shoulders slumped, and he looked at the floor.

"There's nothing like the love of a good woman to soothe the savage beast. Alas, my love was taken from me too quickly, but looking around, I see all manner of potential replacements." He sneered and started a slow and evil laugh. Lindy twisted, rolling toward him, and his knife slipped across the surface of her neck until it was no longer at her throat. She pushed herself away, getting to arm's length before the edge of the blade bit more deeply into her flesh. Rivka fired.

Nefas suddenly gagged, and his arms went limp. Lindy kneed him in the groin before throwing herself backward. Red caught her before she hit the floor. Rivka held the neutron pulse weapon steady. "Oops. It was still set to eleven. You've been judged, you piece of shit."

"Get me the first aid kit!"

Rivka rushed to the bulkhead and pulled the box out. She opened it on the floor.

"Bandages," Red snapped, and held out a hand. She gave him a stack of gauze. Blood flowed freely from the cut in the side of Lindy's neck. Red pressed the bandage down firmly.

"That stings," she said, wincing.

"But it's not your jugular," Red replied softly.

Rivka checked on Jay and Ankh. "What happened?" she asked.

"He came aboard and sprayed something in their faces, then he grabbed me and waited. He only wanted you," Lindy told Rivka.

"They seem fine, just out cold. Where's Lauton?"

"Somebody called?" a tired voice replied. "Hey! What happened here?"

"Do you recognize this guy?" Rivka asked, pointing to Oscura Mandel's body.

"No. Should I?"

"The money laundered through your facility ultimately made it to him."

Lauton sat down next to Rivka on the floor. "Are they okay?" She brushed Jay's hair out of her face.

"They are fine. Knockout spray or something. I have no idea when they'll wake up, but they have strong pulses and are breathing deeply. It's more like they are in a deep sleep. Erasmus, are you there?" Rivka wondered.

"I am. Since I couldn't determine the intruder's actions, I merged with the ship. Chaz and I are sharing cramped quarters. I'll need Ankh's assistance to return to my storage unit."

"Was the box okay when Ankh fell? It wasn't damaged, was it?"

"I don't know. My storage unit is not in the box."

"Where is it? I didn't see Ankh bring anything else aboard."

"It's in his head."

Lindy was sitting up and holding the bandage to her neck while Red went to the galley to get a container of water. Everyone stopped at Erasmus' revelation.

"You fit in there?" Lindy blurted.

"Ankh has a big and beautiful brain."

Rivka coughed. "I suppose he does. When he comes to, we'll do what we need to squeeze you back in there. In the interim, we have some work to do."

Red offered water to Lindy. He stroked her hair with one big hand. "What's up, big guy?" Lindy asked. He shook his head and blinked quickly.

Rivka joined them. "Many people would be traumatized by what you just went through. You seem okay, though. Tell me what you're feeling." The Magistrate touched Lindy's arm and recoiled at the images. "You two!"

Lindy giggled and winked at Red.

"Here you go, Zombie. Touch *my* arm," Red offered.

"No!" the Magistrate shot back, tucking her hands behind her back. "Make sure you're done bleeding before you defile my spaceship."

"Again," Red and Lindy chorused.

"Nothing like a near-death experience to make you feel alive," Lindy added.

"I thought it was just me. I think I've found my soul mate." Red looked adoringly at her.

"You deserve each other." Rivka headed for the bridge. "Erasmus, we need to dig into their digital systems and take them over as the first step toward dismantling them."

"I am at your service, Magistrate," Erasmus replied.

"I may be able to help," Lauton offered. "Should we leave them on the floor?"

Rivka shook her head. "Let's put them in their beds." They took them one by one to their cabins and tucked them in. Red and Lindy went to Red's cabin and closed the door. "Have you seen Hamlet?"

Lauton hadn't. Rivka opened the door to her cabin. Hamlet stood on her pillow and stretched, yawning to show his fangs. He walked in a tight circle and laid back down, smacking his cat lips before closing his eyes.

"Someday, that cat and I are going to have a knock-down drag-out fight."

"It looks like you already have." Lauton looked away from the room. "And lost."

"I haven't had time to clean. Fighting criminals is a full-time job," Rivka tried to explain.

"It's three square meters, but everyone else is earning their keep. Let me clean this up while you get us set up for whatever we need to do for Erasmus."

"*With* Erasmus. You'd do that for me?"

Lauton smiled and nodded. "I'll be done in five minutes."

Rivka thanked her. The sounds coming from Red's quarters convinced her that she needed to be somewhere else.

Anywhere else.

"According to Erasmus, he could find no signs of life in the complex below. I can't believe Nefas and that woman ran everything by themselves. And what's wrong with his ship, that he needed mine?" Rivka spoke out loud as she walked down the stairs. The damage at the bottom was a stark reminder of how they had breached the entry and confronted Nefas.

Rivka stopped when they reached the door. "Wait a moment. I'll let you know when it's clear." Rivka went inside and threw a cover from a couch over the body on the floor. It was starting to smell. When she turned back to call for Lauton, the Zaxxon was already inside and looking at the blanket-covered mound.

"Is that..."

"Yes. I thought I told you to wait," Rivka scolded the woman. "You don't need to see this kind of stuff."

"This is the second dead body I've seen today. My consolation is that it's not me."

"We leave more corpses behind than I had intended when I accepted this position. I'm happy to say they were all guilty of capital crimes. That's how I sleep at night."

Rivka placed coins throughout the room as Erasmus directed her. The datapad provided the interface where he transmitted his instructions.

"Now we wait," Rivka remarked. She looked in the refrigerator to find a stock of beverages and preserved foods. "You'd think he was human, with these tastes."

"He could be a Zaxxon, except he's male."

"Your culture is far different from anything I've seen before. I wish I could have spent more time on your planet to get to know about your people," Rivka replied.

"Maybe when we go back. I hope the planet is back to the way it used to be."

"It will be different. Worse before it gets better, but that's where you come in. You have to help lead the people back to prosperity. Legally, this time."

"But I didn't know!"

"And that's why you haven't been charged. I have judged you innocent."

"That's how it works? You fly in, whip out judgments, kill people, and fly out?"

"That's *not* how it works. We've been on the trail of this one for a while. First and foremost is the law. Upholding Federation law is our charter. The universe is a better place without certain criminals in it. We almost always work with capital crimes, ones where the punishment is death."

Lauton nodded and looked uncomfortable. "How many people have you killed?"

Rivka wanted to answer, but she needed to count. She closed her eyes and sighed. "I don't want to answer that," she finally admitted. "It's not the part of the job I like, although this isn't a job. This is duty to the Federation. It is my way of helping people I will never meet. It's my way of keeping our worlds safe from predators like Oscura Mandel and the Mandolin Partnership. A mandolin is a musical instrument, but it's also a knife."

"I didn't know that," Lauton said, leaning forward with her elbows on her knees and head bowed.

"Criminals think they're smarter than everyone else. They get weird when they find out they're not, either growing ultra-violent as they lash out or being crushed by despair. Nefas was the former."

"Magistrate, I will need you to turn on some of the systems. It appears that there are far more than are currently operating. You'll find the entrance in the seventh alcove from the left."

"Looks like our break is over. We have to answer to our AI master," Rivka quipped. She counted the alcoves until she got to seven and pulled the curtain aside. A locked door greeted them. "Can you unlock the door for us?"

"My lack of fingers makes that quite impossible," Erasmus replied. "Might I suggest a key?"

"I thought you could... Never mind." She pulled her pistol, aimed it at the lock, and fired. The bullet spattered against the metal frame, pinging both the women with shards.

Lauton grimaced and turned away. "I'll wait over here if you don't mind." She plucked small pieces of bullet from her exposed flesh. Blood trickled down her arm.

"Sorry about that," Rivka apologized. She studied the door. It looked as sturdy as the main door that led to the underground. She didn't have Red's main weapon, but he did. "Tell Red to get down here and bring his railgun."

Rivka and Lauton continued exploring while cooling their heels. They found a home that was well cared for. Rivka grabbed a Coke from the refrigerator, offering one to Lauton.

"What is it?" she asked.

"You don't have Coke on Zaxxon Major? Or Pepsi?"

"No. I don't know what they are."

"They are joy in a bottle, and absolutely nothing your body needs. Carbonated sugar-water with flavoring, but oh, so good."

Rivka opened hers and took a long drink. She handed a bottle to Lauton. She opened it and sniffed, then tried to drink it like Rivka had just done. The Magistrate tried to stop her, but it was too late. She gagged, and Coke exploded out her nose, running down her chin and onto her shirt.

She handed the remainder of the bottle to Rivka. "I think I'll pass."

Rivka heard Red's pounding stride before Lauton. "Stand still, so he doesn't do anything funny. He seems to think I'm in trouble."

Lauton stood as still as a statue. Red stopped before he showed himself. The railgun appeared first, then his face.

"We're in here. I need you to open this door."

"That's it? I ran all the way here for that?"

"For fuck's sake, Red, where are your pants?"

"*I thought you were in trouble!* I wished you would have let me know so you didn't come down here alone."

"Lauton is with me," Rivka countered.

"You know what I mean." Red signaled for the women to take cover. "Fire in the hole!"

It didn't take much to blast the door open.

"Damn, I love this thing!" he declared. "Since I'm here, I might as well do my job."

"You look ridiculous," Rivka said of Red's boxers and combat boots.

Red looked hurt. "You have to let me do my job, Magistrate, no matter what else is going on. I can't let any harm come to you. I have a professional reputation to maintain."

Rivka almost touched Red's arm but thought better of it. "I understand. My apologies. You are the best bodyguard I've ever had."

"I'm number one," he replied, knowing that she had never had a bodyguard before him. Red led the way through the alcove and into a room. The railgun had exploded one piece of equipment. Red shrugged. "The door's open."

Rivka looked for power switches, turning on all the gear except the damaged tower. "How's that looking, Erasmus?"

"There should be a main router. Once that's active, I'll be able to access the systems. I can see that they're on, but I can't get inside."

Red, Rivka, and Lauton looked at the only piece of equipment that wasn't powered up. "How can you do it without the router?"

"Ankh would have to physically bypass it by building a secondary router. Why? What's the problem?"

"Your router doesn't appear to have survived the process of breaching the door. Oh well. We'll see you topside." Rivka strolled out, with Red close behind. Lauton followed, not wishing to be left underground.

"That's it? You're giving up?" Red wondered.

"Of course not. I can't build a router. Can you?"

Red shook his head. Lauton shook hers, too.

"We'll let the guy who can build it take care of it. We'll just have to wait. I have a report to write, and we need to prepare to go to Quarst and Belheeake. More evidence to put a bow on this package, but we also need to inform the right people to keep the supply chain from breaking down. I need to call Nathan Lowell and let him know. Maybe the upheaval will be transparent to the end user."

"'Transparent to the end user.' Nice lawyer talk for 'they won't know the difference.'"

"Except that prices may be lower. Maybe…unless budding entrepreneurs are looking to line their pockets with the delta, that is. The difference between the old and new prices."

"We can let people know," Lauton added.

"Knowledge is power," Rivka offered. "Getting you back into your position could be the key to bringing Zaxxon through this. We need to clone you for the other planets."

"I don't want a clone." Lauton looked serious.

"We don't clone people," Red assured her. "She was joking."

"Good. I don't think people should be cloned. That could lead to some very bad things. Can you imagine? Who's that? Lauton Four, not the real Lauton, but she looks like one. No, cloning is a really bad idea. It shouldn't be allowed."

Red mumbled something unintelligible.

Rivka sighed. "There is no cloning of sentient species in the Federation. Relax!"

They walked the rest of the way to the ship in silence.

When they reached the ship, they called Chaz to open the hatch. *New SOP.*

"You go in last. I don't want to see your ass in front of my face."

"I do," Lauton chirped. Rivka pointed for her to go first.

"Next time, I'll tell you, even if you're in the middle of your all-star wrestling match."

"All I ask is the chance to do my job, Magistrate."

"Don't we all, Red? If we only knew exactly what our jobs were, it would be so much easier."

19

Ankh woke up exactly four hours after he'd been knocked out. Jay appeared five minutes later.

"We need to get whatever Mandel used to someone who can reverse engineer it. Four-hour knockout! Be the life of the party..." Red joked.

"That's not a bad idea. We'll turn him over once we get to a Federation station. Ankh, we need you to build a router."

"I feel empty inside," Ankh said in a small voice.

"On that, Erasmus needs your help to get back where he belongs."

"That must happen first," Ankh declared.

Rivka leaned close. "I always assumed that Erasmus was in that bag you carried around. What is in the bag, if it's not him?"

"My stuff." Ankh didn't elaborate.

"Okay," Rivka conceded. "What do you need from us to help you with Erasmus?"

"Peace and quiet."

"Take the bridge." Rivka stood aside to usher Ankh through. Once in, he secured the hatch.

"Chaz," Red began. "What other bars have been programmed into the food thing?"

"Too many to mention. Here's the list." On the screen in the rec room, four columns of menu items appeared.

Red strolled to the dispenser. "Pepperoni pizza roll, cheeseburger, and fudge sundae, please."

The three bars popped out one after the other. Lindy snapped her fingers and pointed to the last bar out. Red looked at it briefly before handing it over. He took a small bite of the pizza roll bar before shoving the whole thing in his mouth.

"I love Ankh," he mumbled while chewing.

The hatch to the bridge opened and Ankh walked out, more upright and confident than before, even though his expression remained as neutral as always.

"Erasmus has made me aware of your problem." The Crenellian closed on Red and stared up at him.

"What?" Red asked. "I love these. You're the best, Ankh."

"Look where you're shooting. You and Terry Henry Walton—blowing stuff up before you know what it is."

"It was behind the door. Door was closed. I opened the door. I apologize for nothing."

"Then *you* fix it, and the food dispenser is getting reprogrammed," Ankh stated flatly.

Red took a knee to be eye-level with the Crenellian. "I am completely ashamed of what I've done. I am sorry, and won't let it happen again."

"I guess that will have to do. Where is this router?"

"Show him, Red. I have reports to write."

Vered stood and turned to Lindy. "Want to see the underground lair?"

"It'll be nice to get off the ship. *Peacekeeper* isn't very big." Lindy held out one hand, and Red slapped a pistol into it. She tucked it into a pocket.

"Follow us, big guy," Red told the small humanoid. Lindy patted his shoulder as she walked past. Ankh trailed them off the ship.

Jay and Rivka looked at each other. "What have you done?" Jay accused. Lauton stayed clear in case there was a fight.

"I think I've created a monster," Rivka admitted. "We have Red, and now we have a female version of Red. Will I be safer with two bodyguards? That's the question."

"What if they have a falling out?" Jay suggested.

"Then we better get some spacesuits so we can abandon ship."

"Probably a wise choice."

"I'll be on the bridge. The reports won't write themselves. I love the law!" Rivka declared as she swaggered to the bridge and jumped into the captain's chair.

"I'm going outside to see the sun. Care to join me?" Jay asked.

"I'd love to." Lauton nodded and followed her out.

Rivka turned her head to watch them go. "All is right with the world when no one is shooting at us," the Magistrate declared. "Okay, Chaz, you and me. Bring up Form 617 stroke 1A, Report of Execution..."

Ankh looked at the router and then at Red. He examined both sides of the tower. "What did you shoot this with?"

Red pointed to his railgun.

"Neanderthal." Ankh had no idea what the term meant, but Ted often used it to describe people who thwarted technological progress.

"We'll be out here if you need us," Red said before leaving the Crenellian to his work. Ankh ignored them and started dismantling the case to see if there was anything he could use.

Red and Lindy went from alcove to alcove, practicing breaching techniques. He gave her the railgun and showed her how to stalk with it, looking over the barrel, making sure it was pointed wherever she looked.

Lindy kept turning her head without moving the railgun.

"It takes a lot of practice." Red tried to be encouraging. It did take a lot of practice to make it a habit.

"Yes, but it cuts reaction time. Makes sense."

"A quick scan. If you want to look around a corner, you dip your head out and pull it back as fast as you can. Your mind will remember what you saw, and you'll present almost no target to your enemy."

She tried that a number of times to get the hang of it. "So much to learn."

"Why do you want to learn it?" Red asked.

"On the ship. When that bastard grabbed me, I didn't know what to do. When you guys were talking with him, it struck me that I'd only get a superficial wound if I turned, and it would give you a free shot. Then I wanted to know more. I never thought about being a warrior, but it seems that the vocation is calling me. I'm never going to wait a table again. I need to learn all the weapons, and more hand-to-hand. No one will ever put me on my heels again. I'll fight back. I may get punched in the face, but I'll fight back."

"My tigress." Red bowed his head to her.

"Rawr," she purred.

Ankh came running from the alcove. "We have to get back to the ship. There's a fleet inbound."

Red tossed the railgun to Lindy and picked up Ankh. They ran up the stairs as fast as their legs would propel them, through the entry and outside, where they found Jay and Lauton lounging. "Into the ship! We gotta go," Red yelled as he ran past. Lindy waved at them to hurry.

Jay was up in an instant. Lauton hesitated, but Jay pulled her to her feet and propelled her toward the stairs.

Once they were inside, Red secured the hatch.

"Buckle up so we can take off!" Rivka shouted from the bridge. The crew jumped into their seats. Before they were strapped in, the ship launched from the ground and raced skyward.

"Erasmus will operate the shields and weapon systems," Ankh said.

"Did you get done what you needed?" Red asked.

"Yes." Ankh's eyes lost focus and he assumed his blank stare, closely engaged with Erasmus. He hugged his pack to his chest.

"Someone must have stolen his toys when he was a child," Lindy suggested.

"I wonder what it's all about, but I'm not going to be the one who violates his trust." He indicated the bag with his eyes.

"Not me! He can probably kill me with his brain." Lindy shook her finger at Red. "Shame on you."

"Don't look at me!" Jay shot an angry look Red's way. He smiled back and shook his head.

"I wouldn't do that, Jay. Leave Ankh be. He's already saved us once. That's why I'm not worried now."

"*I am*," Lauton exclaimed, eyes wide in terror as the ship continued its steep ascent. It powered through the upper atmosphere and immediately started dodging. They could hear the weapons discharges.

"Hang on!" Rivka yelled from the bridge.

Red started to question his faith in their survival. "Fuck me! Just when my life was on track."

Lindy chuckled and stretched her arm toward the big bodyguard. They held hands and smiled.

"That's it? You're going to hold hands while we're about to *die*?" Lauton's words spilled from her in a rush.

"As part of this crew, I've learned two things." Lindy hesitated as the ship bucked and the lights flickered. "Don't waste time worrying about what's not in your control, and trust your teammates."

Peacekeeper spiraled one way before jerking and diving. It bumped and screamed as it reentered the upper atmosphere.

"Fuck you!" Rivka shouted through clenched teeth, giving the double bird to the main screen. She was jerked back and forth even in the captain's well-padded chair. The screen to the left showed the pirate fleet on the tactical display.

"That's your secret, you bastard," Rivka growled. The screen showed nine frigate-class ships and a massive brute that probably carried the last of the fighters from the Ixtali War. "I knew there should have been more. That was how you brought the planets under your umbrella. They had no way to defend themselves from your fleet, because they didn't have one. Then you'd use your wealth to buy your way across the galaxy."

The corvette continued into the atmosphere, but none of the ships followed. The tactical display showed ten ships in orbit, with a squadron of the old fighters detaching from the carrier.

"Erasmus, tell me that we can hold our own against those fighters."

"I will tell you that if you would like, but it wouldn't be the truth," the AI replied.

"Thanks for the honesty. Are we better off fighting them within the planet's atmosphere?"

"Yes. Their weaponry is most effective in the near-vacuum of space." The ship slowed significantly and reoriented upward. "They will lose maneuverability during reentry. I will eliminate as many of them as possible during that transition."

Rivka nodded, her knuckles white from gripping her armrests. Her gaze darted back and forth between the main screen and tactical. The ship accelerated upward as if launched by a rocket. The corvette's small railguns sent streams of projectiles toward unseen targets. The main screen showed the dark blue of a transitioning sky. Rivka could see nothing specific. Erasmus continued accelerating, firing as he went. Two missiles detached from the ship and raced away, then two more.

"How many missiles do we have left? Are we going to be able to survive the next fight without them?"

"If we don't survive this fight, Magistrate, the next one is irrelevant."

Tiny explosions dotted the main screen before the view changed. *Peacekeeper* began running parallel to the planet. The remaining fighters quickly overshot the corvette as they attempted to slow.

Erasmus swung the ship around, firing at the fighters from a distance. One more died before the single-person ships regained their maneuverability and started to spread out.

"Four left," Rivka muttered to herself. The corvette headed straight for them. The gravitic shields had not been challenged by the fighters' weapons. Erasmus planned on them holding, hoping that the fighters had not been reconfigured with more powerful weaponry than what the ships had carried during the war.

The last four fighters approached from different vectors. *Peacekeeper* fired and maneuvered. Their plasma weapons bracketed the corvette as they closed. Some splashed off the shields.

"So far so good," Rivka whispered.

The screen whited out with a sparkling flash before returning. Rivka's modified eyes adjusted quickly. The screen showed the fighters skipping by on their high-speed passes. The last two missiles launched into the path of the incoming vessels, too quickly for them to maneuver. *Peacekeeper* was buffeted by the explosions. The corvette tipped on its side as its thrusters attempted to drive a sharper turn.

The fighters jetted skyward, disengaging. The corvette slowed.

"I'd say chase them, but that's Angry Me talking and not Smart Me."

"Smart You is aligned with Smart Me," Erasmus replied.

Rivka unbuckled herself and left the bridge. "Everyone okay back here?"

"Did we win?" Red asked.

"We won a reprieve, or maybe it's a stay of execution. I believe this fleet has orders to kill us, so it's probably not a stay." Rivka made a fist and hammered it on the table. "I've had about enough of the Mandolin fucking Partnership."

"Maybe we can tell them he is no more and that they won't be getting paid?" Jay suggested.

"They already want to kill us, so it can't hurt. Erasmus, can you craft a message? Include pictures of his corpse, and transmit to their fleet."

"Done," Erasmus replied almost instantly.

"And they are starting to move away..." Rivka let it hang as if Erasmus would confirm her hopes.

"None of the ships are showing any inclination to leave orbit."

"Keep transmitting. Maybe it'll get through their thick heads that they won't be able to replace what they lose since they won't be getting paid!" Rivka leaned against the galley counter.

"Ankh programmed lots of good eats into our hooya there," Red stated, pointing with a tip of his chin. "If I get too technical, stop me."

Rivka shook her head as she looked at her crew. "Keep up your good spirits. We're going to need them before this is all over. What should I order?"

"Pepperoni pizza roll or turkey and stuffing. It's hard not to find something that's great. Except that Vegemite sandwich thing. That made me gag, but I showed it who was boss."

"How many of the new bars did you eat?"

"All of them!" Lindy interjected.

"Not *all*," Red clarified.

Rivka ordered one each of the first two and avoided the third. "What's your plan, Erasmus?"

Ankh stood and stretched. "We will land and attempt to get the other ship airborne. If it can provide enough of a distraction, we may be able to clear the atmosphere long enough to gate out of here," the Crenellian stated, not talking to anyone in particular and not asking permission.

The Magistrate didn't need him to ask. It was their only plan. She took her two bars and returned to the bridge. "Chaz, please connect me to Nathan Lowell."

"Normal communication is not possible because of interference from the ships in orbit."

"Surely that doesn't affect the Interstellar communication system?"

"It does not, but our ICS is not currently functional."

"Why is that? We didn't take any damage from the enemy fleet."

"Ankh used some of the components to bring the Mandolin systems online. Do you want evidence, or do you want communication? Ankh can probably put the ICS back together, but it will take some time since *Peacekeeper* lacks a proper workshop. We got the evidence, Magistrate. It is all that you hoped for."

"I guess there's that. We have enough to convict the guy that's already dead without dissuading those who are fighting on his behalf. I think I now have a better grasp of what a Pyrrhic victory means. Did my report get through, at least?"

"It did not," Erasmus answered.

"It was incomplete anyway. Please add the new evidence into the file. I'll resend when I've touched it up."

"When will you do that?" Erasmus asked.

"When we're not about to die."

"When will that be?"

"Judging from my experience as a Magistrate, that will be the Fourth of Never in the month of Not Now. Fine. I'll work on it while you and Ankh are trying to figure out what's wrong with that other ship."

"We could use a hand," Ankh requested from the corridor outside the bridge. Rivka looked past him.

"Anyone know anything about starships?"

No one said yes.

"I'm willing to learn, if that matters," Lauton offered.

"You go with Ankh when we touch down. And Ankh?" The Crenellian's big head turned but stopped before they made eye contact. "Thank you for reprogramming the food dispenser. You've made this trip much more enjoyable, along with saving our lives on a couple of occasions. I won't forget that."

Ankh didn't reply. He headed to the exit and waited for the ship to land.

20

"Are we at an impasse?" Rivka asked.

"I don't understand," Chaz replied.

"They stay up there, we stay down here. It's an impasse, but one I'll take since the alternative is, we fight ten ships that are all bigger and better armed than we are."

"I expect they are discussing the situation. The nine frigates are all capable of flying within the atmosphere."

"Then why don't they come after us?"

"It would leave a gap in their jamming, and we'd be able to broadcast a message."

"Why would they worry about that? They come down here, kill us, and move on before any help can arrive."

"Maybe they feel information has been compromised regarding their fleet, possibly their home base, suppliers, communication protocols, methodologies for selecting targets, and so on. There is a great deal of information that could be harmful to their continued existence."

"That sounds as plausible as anything. Do you know what Ankh's status is?"

"Erasmus reports that they've found the problem. There are two major failures in the ship, both engine-related. The first can be fixed, but the second would require one of the miniaturized Etheric power supplies."

"I don't think we can give either one of them up, which means the dead ship stays dead. Tell Ankh to come on back."

"Would you like us to recover the components from the ICS?"

Rivka checked the tactical display to confirm they weren't under threat. "Yes, and take Red with you."

Lindy got up from her seat, but Rivka shook her head. "We'll keep half here and half outside the ship. Then if anything horrible happens, we don't have all our eggs in one basket, as it may be. You can be my bodyguard in Red's absence if he'll trust you with the job."

Red rushed to the storage locker. He pulled an extra railgun out and told it to receive programming. He handed it to Lindy, who wrapped her palm and fingers around the grip.

A blip of a green light showed that the weapon had integrated Lindy as a user. "Take care of the Magistrate for me while I'm gone." Red checked his gear one more time and ran off the ship. Lindy followed him to the hatch, then took a seat in the entry, her feet on the top step as she noted her surroundings, creating a baseline image in her mind, any deviation from which would be cause for alarm.

Rivka returned to the bridge and brought up her report.

Red, Ankh, and Lauton had been inside for a total of ten seconds when Chaz shouted, "Incoming!"

"Where?" Rivka asked in surprise. The tactical display showed ships in orbit.

Lindy prepared to run after Red and the others, but they had already reappeared and were sprinting toward the corvette. Red carried Ankh and Lauton tried to keep up. A fireball raced through the sky, headed directly for them.

Red sped up. Lauton put on a burst of speed, and they arrived at the ship within a half-second of each other. Once inside, Lindy slapped the red button. *Peacekeeper* was already on the move while the stairs retracted and the hatch closed. The ship bolted away from the compound as the violence of an orbital delivery rocked the ground, destroying Nefas' ship.

The blast and shockwave would have destroyed *Peacekeeper* had she still been there.

"A frigate has entered the atmosphere and is in pursuit," Chaz reported. "Erasmus is taking over the engagement."

Chaz went silent, as he did when the ship was in a fight. Erasmus was the combat expert, due to the experience that the AIs in his lineage had shared with him. The ship turned sharply, fired, and dashed away.

The crew fought to gain their seats and strap themselves in.

"A second frigate is entering the upper atmosphere."

"I guess they aren't afraid of compromising videos," Rivka suggested from her seat on the bridge.

"Or they figured out we are running silent."

"I really hate these guys," Rivka muttered before yelling at the enemy ship's image on the main screen. "Let it go!"

The enemy wasn't listening. The corvette screeched in agony from a direct hit. Erasmus conducted a series of erratic maneuvers attempting to shape the engagement in a way most favorable to the corvette's weapon systems. *Peacekeeper* adjusted one last time. Rivka gripped the armrests and pressed back into the seat.

"I got a bad feeling..." she started to say.

"Gate forming," Erasmus reported calmly.

"Inside the atmosphere?" Red roared.

The Gate sparked and danced, solid but not. The corvette stopped before entering and started accelerating backward. The event horizon collapsed, dragging atmosphere in and kicking it back out. The explosion tore one frigate in half.

BOOM! Smoke filled the inside of *Peacekeeper* after the explosion. Fire control systems activated in the engine compartment and the ship started to drop. Thrusters kicked in to stabilize it as the gravitic engines, after an emergency shutdown, came back to life. The ship started to accelerate. The air handling system kicked into over-drive to clear the air.

"Talk to me," Rivka ordered her ship.

"The Gate engine and one Etheric power supply have been destroyed," Erasmus reported. The ship nosed up and rolled over. The weapons fired as the corvette darted toward the enemy. *Peacekeeper* heeled over, buffeted by the explosion from the second frigate.

"Tactical shows clear," Rivka reported. "What's the chance of us surviving another attack?"

"You don't want to know the odds. Suffice it to say they aren't good."

"And without our Gate drive, the gap in the orbits

doesn't matter. We can't talk to anyone. We can't fly out of here. We're out of missiles. Give me some options, people."

"Blaze of glory." Red clearly enunciated each word. Lindy nodded. Tears ran down Jay's face.

"What does that mean? I'm a hostage on this ship! Let me off before you do anything stupid," Lauton demanded.

"Jay, I'll need you to get off the ship, too. Someone has to look after Lauton." Rivka thought for a moment. "And take Hamlet with you. He doesn't need to suffer for our failures. Ankh?"

"As long as there is a greater than zero chance of survival, we have a chance. As long as Erasmus and I are with you, that chance improves exponentially."

"That sounds like good news, Ankh. Does that mean you know how we can replace our missiles?"

Ankh didn't dignify that with an answer. He sat silently, looking at nothing but seeing everything.

"Take us to the compound," Rivka ordered whichever entity happened to be flying the ship at the moment. The corvette assumed a leisurely pace and angle of descent. When it landed, Jay already had her things. Lauton took Jay's bundle so she could pick up Hamlet and carry him off the ship. He started to fight when he saw the door, but Jay clamped down hard. He hissed, but let her leave the ship with him.

No one said goodbye. The hatch closed. Lindy and Red embraced, holding each other as if there would be no tomorrow. Ankh was lost in thought with Erasmus. Rivka gently pushed the couple, encouraging them toward their seats. The thoughts she intruded on were of pure love.

Tears filled her eyes. She tried to blink them away, but they kept coming.

"Take your seats, guys," she told them before going to the bridge, indifferent to whether they sat or not.

"Chaz, record a message to be jettisoned upon our destruction. Include all the evidence, my report, Ankh's reports, and the following for Nathan Lowell. 'Nathan, please do everything you can to fill the vacuum that Mandolin's demise created. We want the least amount of negative impact on the good people of those planets who never knew what was going on. They are the ones we're fighting and dying for.'

"For Grainger. 'I appreciate everything you taught me and tried to teach me. Sometimes, even when you have the right answer, things don't go your way. Peace, my brother. I hope to see you again when the Etheric pukes up the dead. You'll owe me about a bazillion beers by then. Pay up, bitch, or I'll haunt you. Tell the others I'm going to miss them. And most of all, thanks for hiring Vered. He's a loyal and good friend.'

"Take us out. Let's see how many of those bastards we can take with us. What do you say we hedge our bet by skimming the upper atmosphere and seeing what kind of response we can evoke?"

"Yes, Magistrate," Erasmus replied. *Peacekeeper* lifted away from Nefas' building and slowly climbed into the air.

"It's Judgment Day," she whispered.

At slow cruise, the ship was quiet. Nothing distracted anyone from their thoughts. "I never got to fire my rail-gun," Lindy lamented.

Red didn't answer.

Peacekeeper touched the upper atmosphere, where the sky turned from light to dark blue and then to black.

The enemy frigates created a basket around the corvette. *Erasmus* dove back into the atmosphere and accelerated. The ships in orbit easily kept pace. The corvette made a tight turn and redlined the acceleration. The ship raced out from under the basket and screamed upward and into space.

Defensive weapons engaged and the ship rotated through a three-sixty, grazing the enemy formation with railgun and plasma fire. One of the frigates' shields failed. The impacts penetrated the ship, and it vented air. It dropped out of the race. The other ships sped up, surrounding *Peacekeeper*. All weapons fired.

"Like Chosin Reservoir, we have the enemy right where we want him. No matter which way we fire, we'll hit the bastards," Erasmus intoned.

Beyond the largest of the enemy ships, the bright light of a Gate formed.

Erasmus spoke evenly, as he always did. "The *War Axe*."

"Fire the mains," Captain Micky San Marino barked. The special railguns arranged from stem to stern were able to accelerate projectiles to near lightspeed. On rapid fire at close range, it was like getting hit by so many nuclear weapons. The enemy carrier shattered as if made of glass. Minor explosions disappeared quickly as the air became one with the vastness of space. Three frigates were vaporized before they realized a new enemy had appeared. Two more died when they turned to fight. Another died when it tried to run. The last one skipped off the upper atmosphere, using maximum acceleration to slingshot around the planet and head into deep space.

Without an integral Gate, it was years from reappearing, if it reappeared at all. The Gate in the system would have to be monitored to prevent the pirate frigate from using it. Or Ankh and Ted could turn it off, only to be reactivated by use of a Federation code.

It would be years before any last holdouts from Mandolin reared their ugly heads.

"Nice shooting," Micky told his ship. "Get me that corvette, Smedley."

"My compliments to your timing, Captain," Rivka replied to the call.

Terry Henry pumped his fist. "Two wins in one day. You're going to spoil me, Skipper."

"Let's not do too much more of that." Micky's words were harsh, but he nodded and smiled.

"We've lost our Gate drive and one of our power supplies, and we left two people on the planet we need to pick up."

"Your final message has been transmitted," Erasmus' voice could be heard over Rivka's open microphone.

"What? That was only if we died. We didn't die. You have to get it back!"

"No can do, Magistrate," the AI replied.

"Ankh!" she yelled.

"Do you need an escort to the planet's surface, Magistrate?"

"Oh, shit. You heard that? Never mind. Yes, we would

like a ride if you can swing it. Open those big-ass doors of yours. Our ship needs a little work, and probably a new coat of paint, too."

Terry spoke loudly to make sure that Rivka could hear. "How is this lawyer thing working out for you, Barrister?" Char punched him in the arm.

"Ignore him," she told the Magistrate. "We appreciate the job you do. Micky's giving me the thumbs-up. Doors are opening. Relinquish thruster control to Smedley, please."

"What happened with the phantom destroyer and Keeg Station?" Rivka asked while docking procedures were underway.

"That's a story for a different day," Colonel Terry Henry Walton replied.

21

The *War Axe* set down on the apron before the lone building. The airlock next to the hangar doors opened, and Rivka and her crew walked out into the daylight.

"How long have we been here?" Red asked. No one knew. "I'll be damned. I guess time *does* fly when you're having fun!"

"Don't talk to me." Rivka shook a warning finger at him.

"Lighten up, Magistrate. If we aren't near death every ten minutes, we'd all get bored. It wouldn't be us without explosions."

"That's what scares me, Red. We expend a lot of ordnance on these missions. Damn! I called it a mission and not a case. Next time, Grainger, I want a case!"

Jay and Lauton waved from the entryway before jogging toward the team.

Red turned to Lindy and rolled his eyes. She started to laugh.

"We leave you for five minutes, and Red eats so much you have to get a bigger ship," Jay quipped.

"Hey! How did I get drug into this?"

"Because you're the only male here," Lindy replied. Red pointed a big finger at the cat. "Does he even have his balls?"

"Whoa!" Red held up a hand. "That gives me the willies. Is this case wrapped up, Magistrate?"

"I think so. Why do you ask?"

"When Grainger first hired me, he said that if I could keep you alive through three missions, he'd give me a bonus. I thought it would be the easiest money I ever made."

Rivka sneered. "Was it?"

"No. It sucked, but you're still alive, so maybe if you take some time off, Lindy and I can take a vacation to the pleasure moon of Titan with my extensive wealth."

"How much did he promise you?"

"He made me swear not to tell you."

"Grainger is a dead man. He didn't think I would survive three cases?"

"To your earlier point, he called them missions."

"How is Floyd?" Jay asked.

"Haven't seen him yet," Lindy replied.

"What are we waiting for?" Jay prodded.

Rivka shrugged and waved them ahead. Once on board, the destroyer took off and headed for space.

"Do you have everything?" Jay asked for the third time.

"Yes," Lauton replied impatiently. *Peacekeeper* landed in the area outside her home. They expected to see the building burned to the ground, but it was intact. Red and Lindy accompanied Jay and Lauton, while Rivka watched from the bridge. Ankh and Erasmus were pleased to find that they still had access to the systems on Zaxxon Major, so they were on a digital exploration.

The home had been ransacked, but nothing she needed or wanted had been taken. "I'll get this cleaned up in no time. What do I do tomorrow?" she wondered.

"Go to work, take your old job, and start working toward an ethical solution to your planet's problems. The prosperity you enjoyed was artificial, but if it could be exploited while also being beneficial, the potential is extraordinary." Rivka had been talking with Ankh and used his words.

"I think it has the potential, too. It's my home." Everyone stood around uncomfortably until Red stepped up.

"Time to go."

Jay hugged Lauton intensely, and then they kissed.

"I'll be in my bunk," Red said, eliciting an elbow nudge from Lindy. With Rivka in the lead, they headed back to the ship. "Would you look at that?"

"What?" Lindy asked, head swiveling as she tried to find what had caught Red's attention. Rivka looked over her shoulder, curious as well.

"We're not running."

"Gate drive is replaced, and a new secondary power supply is installed. Don't blow this one, please. I don't have any more!" Ted warned Ankh.

"We had no choice. In Erasmus' opinion, it was the greatest chance for survival. The end result suggests that he was correct."

"Fine, fine," Ted argued. "But don't do it again or you'll be dead. Your ship needs to have independent Gating ability."

"I understand," Ankh replied. "We shall endeavor to persevere."

"So you're going to stay with them?" Ted observed.

"They eat well. My cabin is comfortable, and most importantly, they need me."

"Make sure they treat you as an equal and not a servant."

"I understand," Ankh repeated.

"Take care of yourself, Ankh. And them. I get the impression from Terry and Char that they like the Magistrate, and would be quite upset if any harm came to her."

"They won't realize how much I will do for them, but I will do it because you ask."

"They never realize, Ankh, but they *do* appreciate it. Accept that they don't know the extent of what we do, because they cannot know. Their minds haven't gone where ours can."

The Crenellian maintained his expressionless look, needing to say nothing further. They stood like that for a few moments before each going their own way. Ted disappeared through the hatch to the interior of the destroyer.

A fire team of Bad Company warriors showed up, each of the four carrying a bulky crate.

"Where's that going to go?"

"Spare parts go into storage, and I will modify the extra cabin to be a workroom."

Rivka didn't want to hold the Crenellian back. "Welcome aboard, Ankh, and thanks for joining the team."

He looked at her for a moment before heading into the ship.

"What do you think is on his mind when he does that?" Jay asked.

"Not a clue, but we all have our quirks."

Jay faced the Magistrate. "We all have our unique way of approaching life." Jay shook her rainbow-colored hair.

"That's a much better way of looking at it." Rivka turned serious. "Are you staying on with the crew?"

"Things are just getting interesting. Now is not the time to leave. I'll stay for as long as you'll have me."

"Then we better get you some time in the Pod-doc."

"It won't change me, will it?" Jay worried.

"It will change some of your physical characteristics, but we're up here, aren't we?" Rivka tapped her temple with a finger. "Stress is a window to the soul. Same thing with success. Do your looks define you, or is it what you do? Words only matter when followed by action."

"Words alone can tear people apart," Jay suggested, sadness tinging her voice.

"And that's why you're a member of the team. You bring a perspective that the rest of us don't have."

Jay smiled briefly and, lost in her thoughts, made her way on board. The hangar bay was mostly empty and quiet. The work on the corvette had been completed, the equipment stored, and the maintenance bots recovered to do other work for the *War Axe*.

Red, Christina, and Kai appeared from the doors that led to the armory. They each carried boxes.

"Where are we going to put that?" Rivka exclaimed. "And what did you do with Lindy?"

Red smiled and waggled his eyebrows, his bald head shiny under the lights. A heavy mechanical tread resounded from the doorway, and a mechanized combat suit appeared. The faceplate was mirrored, but Rivka knew who was driving it.

"Don't tell me you're borrowing a mech?"

"You can have it," Christina replied.

Lindy hoisted the mech-sized railgun into the air.

"Where are we going to put the mech? Come on, Red, I'm a lawyer! I think you have the wrong idea about what we do."

Red looked confused. "Magistrate, I've been with you on every one of your missions. Some need the mech more than others, but better to have it and not need it, right?"

"I have the law on my side!" Rivka declared. Red motioned with his head to deliver the new load of weaponry, ammunition, and explosives.

"How'd that work out on Morinvaille?"

"A mech would have come in handy. And explosives. Fine. Bring the mech."

"You can strap it on the outside of the ship. You don't need to keep it inside," Christina explained. They handed the boxes to the warriors leaving the ship after delivering

Ankh's crates. The four took the three boxes and hurried inside.

"Put them in the rec room," Red shouted after them. One of the warriors was bleeding from a long scratch down his arm. "And watch out for that cat. He's a ruthless killer."

"Don't I know it," the man said over his shoulder.

Terry and Char strode briskly across the hangar deck, the wombat's long nails clicking on the metal as she trundled after them. "We're glad we caught you." Terry offered his hand, and they shook. Char hugged her. "Sorry. I guess we're not supposed to touch you, but I've had other people inside my head for as long as I can remember." He pointed at Char with his thumb.

"I don't. He's simply transparent. Anyone can see what he's thinking," Char clarified. Rivka had seen into both their minds and found it refreshing. No subterfuge. No hidden agendas. No secrets that they were trying to hide.

"You should think about becoming a Magistrate. Both of you."

"What, and leave all this behind? We will continue our life's work rescuing Magistrates. And the downtrodden—we'll help them, too," Terry explained.

Is Jay here? a small voice asked in Rivka's mind.

"She's inside," Rivka answered, looking for the source of the question. Floyd wobbled past and bounced up the stairs and into the ship.

"What the..."

"We put her in the Pod-doc. She's like a small child. Plenty smart. I wish she would stop with the marking her territory. She is adamant about it."

"Marking?"

"You don't want to know. We have a bot follow us around for the sole purpose of cleaning up after her." Terry pointed to the small bot hovering inside the hatch on the side of the bay.

Char leaned close to the Magistrate.

"I think Terry likes blowing stuff up too much to do anything else. After a century and a half, one gets set in their ways. We'll stay with the Bad Company and do our best to keep the Federation at peace, in our own way. You do it your way, and in the end, we'll all get to live in a better place." Char smiled, took Terry's hand, and waved goodbye. "Oh, Nathan wants to talk with you."

Rivka waved back and hurried into the ship, working her way around the various crates and bags filling the corridors.

"This looks like a Rigellian pirate freighter! I'm not cleaning it up, but *someone* sure as hell is," Rivka bellowed from the bridge before securing the hatch behind her. A soft meow came from under the front console. "Hamlet. What are you doing in here? Are there too many changes for my little introvert? Come up here and give me some loving."

Surprisingly, the cat climbed from his hiding spot and leapt into her lap, lying down as she stroked his fur.

"Chaz, connect me to Nathan Lowell, please."

The screen shimmered to life, and Nathan appeared with a distinguished-looking older man, with gray at his temples and a cigar in his mouth. The father of the Queen.

"Nathan, Lance, nice to see you both." Rivka wanted to talk about the twenty planets that had been freed from the

Mandolin Partnership, but didn't want to interfere with her boss's boss's boss's agenda.

"Once again, good work, Rivka." Nathan smiled broadly and nodded once.

Lance Reynolds, nominal head of the Federation, chimed in, "I am impressed that you were able to dismantle a major corporation like that. I think I need to be more clear when I send guidance. You were only supposed to collect evidence and determine if there was more. You were never supposed to engage with someone who had their own combat fleet and billions of credits worth of influence. In any case, I like your can-do attitude, Magistrate. My daughter was right about you."

"I don't know what to say," Rivka replied.

"You don't need to say anything. I'd love to give you lots of time off to recover, but criminals won't take a day off, so the good must be vigilant. Get back to Station 7 and get your people into the Pod-doc. Get your upgrades, and then take your new mission. It'll take you a week to prep for it, but we need you out there on the front lines defending the good people of the Federation from criminals like Oscura Mandel."

"There are more criminals like him?"

"Different criminals, but there will always be someone who wants to be the next Mandolin. The lure of money and power makes people take obscene risks and do weird things. Magistrates can stop that cold, but only if they're out there. I'm sorry, Rivka for asking you to remain constantly deployed. Remember, evil never sleeps."

"There is a blood trade out here. Mandel was a buyer to use as leverage over world leaders. Maybe in the data we'll find who the supplier was, but as of right now, it's still out there. I'll let the other Magistrates know. We'll end the blood trade, one way or another.

Nathan said a few last words. "We would all appreciate that, Rivka. On another note, Lance has approved bonuses for your crew. Are you going to add any more people? If so, we'll have to talk about your budget in greater detail."

Rivka didn't bother to mention the bonus she was going to give her crew as part of her winnings from Red's victory in the fight on S'Korr. She opened the hatch to show the current state of her ship. "We are packed to the gills. That's it on crew. It'll only be the five of us."

"Looks like six," Nathan said, pointing at the cat in Rivka's lap. "If you want the whole Evil Magistrate vibe, you'll have to get a hairless cat."

"I'm not getting another cat. I didn't even want this one."

"That's the thing about cats, Magistrate. We don't choose them, they choose us. Lowell out."

"Is that how it works, little man?" Rivka asked. He was purring rhythmically in response to being petted. "Chaz, make sure we don't have any stragglers on board, like warriors or wombats, and let's take to the sky. Sounds like we have a new case."

Grainger looked at Rivka over a pile of plates. He stifled a belch. She ducked her head and did the same thing. "So..." He didn't finish the sentence.

"You weren't clear at all on the job description, bitch," she accused.

"Your alternatives were limited. Remember that part where you were in prison garb and shackles? Did the job description matter?"

Rivka chewed on her lip. Her stomach grumbled. "Happy tummy," she purred. "I guess not. Will people be trying to kill me everywhere I go? I now have powered armor and major firepower on board my corvette. Hello, my name is Rivka Anoa. You're innocent until proven guilty, except that you're really not. Don't look at the mech or she'll kill you, just like I will."

"Sounds legit. Maybe you should start more conversations that way."

"You didn't feed me and then say such nice things because I was hungry." Rivka leaned back and crossed her arms.

"Your next mission—" Grainger started.

"Case," Rivka corrected.

"Mission."

"*Case*."

"Your next foray to shine light into the dark places of our galaxy is a serial killer on Collum."

"Serial killers fall under local jurisdiction. They suck, but they aren't a Federation issue."

"Unless they are only killing foreign dignitaries. We've lost one a week for the last eight weeks. It can't continue, or all the delegations will pull out. You know what the Federation thinks about having to abandon a planet, plus Collum's Chancellor has requested Federation intervention."

"This sounds more like a normal case. Do they have any suspects?"

"Some, but none sound promising. Everything we have is in the case file. Download it before you go. And on a separate note, your death message was touching."

"That was sent by mistake. I think Erasmus was trying to get back at me for being taller than his Crenellian."

"I'm sure that's it." Grainger stood and almost bumped into Doctor Tyler Toofakre. "Excuse me," he said before turning back to Rivka. "You don't need to leave for a couple days. They're expecting you on Thursday. Enjoy your downtime."

"I'm sorry I'm late. Emergency dental repair. A front tooth had been knocked out, but she wouldn't say what the circumstances were. Oh! You've already eaten."

"You think domestic abuse?" Rivka asked, suddenly interested.

"I don't know." He waved to get the server's attention and ordered the same thing he always ordered. "I am concerned. Don't look, but there she is now. Is that your bodyguard?"

Lindy and Red both waved.

Rivka started to laugh and motioned for them to come into All Guns Blazing's restaurant.

"You know her?" Tyler asked.

"Quite well, as a matter of fact. I have my suspicions about what happened." When Lindy and Red arrived, Rivka fixed them with a stare. "Let me guess—you were testing how well your new nanocytes made repairs. Didn't he tell you that the first pass isn't good with teeth? It'll take another time or two before the nanos figure out how to fix a chipped tooth."

Lindy punched Red in the shoulder. "Dammit!"

Red tried to look innocent, pointing at Lindy and then at his arm.

"How do you know about the teeth?" Lindy wondered.

"He fixed mine too." Rivka nodded to the dentist.

"Thanks for taking care of me, doc. I have to admit, I expected weird. Seriously, who likes sticking their meat hooks into someone else's mouth? But you're a normal guy. You know what? With us around, she needs more normal in her life."

Tyler didn't know how to respond to that. Rivka let him off the hook.

Rivka frowned. "Next case is on Collum. We're going after a serial killer who's hunting aliens."

"The hunter becomes the hunted. We got your back, Magistrate," Red promised.

The End

Destroy the Corrupt - Judge, Jury, & Executioner, Book 2

If you like this book, please leave a review. This is a new series, so the only way I can decide whether to commit more time to it is by getting feedback from you, the readers. Your opinion matters to me. Continue or not? I have only so much time to craft new stories. Help me invest that time wisely. Plus, reviews buoy my spirits and stoke the fires of creativity.

Don't stop now! Keep turning the pages as Craig & Michael talk about their thoughts on this book and the overall project called the Age of Expansion.
Your new favorite legal eagle will return in Book 3, *Serial Killer*!

You are still reading! Thank you so much. It doesn't get much better than that.

My Bad Company Book 3 – *Price of Freedom* is a finalist for the Dragon Award for the best Military Science Fiction of the year! At first, I didn't care, but then I talked to a few people, and it is a big deal. Who skips the Academy Awards? Well, it wasn't going to be me, so I bought my ticket and am going to Atlanta to attend a couple days of DragonCon and the award ceremony. We have a lot of work to do between now and then to rally the vote. I don't want to go all that way and not win, do I?

Michael Anderle will be there too, and we'll be on stage together. I would love to win, and hope that you signed up to vote (before this book comes out) and that you voted after you received your ballot. We appreciate your support, first and foremost as readers who enjoy our stories.

I have a copy of Black's *Law Dictionary*, and that is my main reference. The law is incredibly complex, and ninety percent of a lawyer's job is looking stuff up. Research, research, research. The shows on TV show the cool lawyers whipping things off the top of their heads, quoting legal precedent by case name. They only get there by studying and memorizing—the oft-maligned Socratic method, as it may be. Yes, law school is where you earn your stripes in figuring out how to research, and coherently defend a position based on that research. Nothing is cut and dried. In law school, we had to take one position, switch sides, and then defend the other position with equal zeal. That's where lawyers in training learn the ropes.

Veronica Helen's Kingpin's name:

Oscura (Italian for dark)

Nefas (Latin origins of nefarious)

Organization name: Nefas Services

Micky Cocker – Mandolin Inc, but I went with Partnership as offered by Staci Armstrong. (Kitchen slicer or musical instrument, a double entendre)

And Oscura Mandel as the nominal head. I am at the point where I had to choose the names—look for a mash-up of a number of offerings—thanks to Staci Armstrong, James Caplan, Micky Cocker, and Veronica Helen for their suggestions. We'll find the Mandolin Partnership (there's a twist here, you'll have to read the book) with nominal head Oscura Mandel. He goes by Nefas, his middle name, but only to his friends. Are you my friend, Rivka?

Here are some of the other offerings for names and such. Thank you to such a great group of supporters.

Tommy Donbavand offered a couple names that I used in this book—go Tommy D!

Zaxxon Major—six continents, constantly at war with each other

Quarst—small world with 124 smaller moons surrounding it

Micky Cocker offered the following names that all appear somewhere within *Destroy the Corrupt*. Gargeath, Kleath, Lauton, Colston, Dromet, Reemstar,

Breedin. Rashveil, Solaric, Pyrothasm, Collum Gate and Morinvaille. For the record, every time I referenced the planet called Morinvaille, I copied it and pasted it from a previous entry.

Jordan Smith suggested Show Low—named after a poker game, someone gambled the planet and showed the lowest card to win. This planet plays a small role in the book:)

Heidi Bauer suggested a name that I used—I like it, but it was hard to type. You'll see that I often try to keep things simple for the sake of my fingers and typing speed. Belheeake

Tom Dickerson suggested S'Korr, a sports arena-type planetary economy with overpriced beverages and snacks, plus cheap team-logo knickknacks.

There was a great thread in the Kurtherian Fans group offering names and planets and races, with the accompanying background data. I have these suggestions already copied over and will be using more of them. Thank you to everyone who dropped a few lines for me.

I hope everyone enjoyed this story. It was fun to write in a way that I found most relaxing.

Peace, fellow humans.

Please join my Newsletter (www.craigmartelle.com – please, please, please sign up!), or you can follow me on Facebook since you'll get the same opportunity to pick up the books for only 99 cents on that first day they are published.

If you liked this story, you might like some of my other books. You can join my mailing list by dropping by my website **www.craigmartelle.com** or if you have any comments, shoot me a note at craig@craigmartelle.com. I am always happy to hear from people who've read my work. I try to answer every email I receive.

If you liked the story, please write a short review for me on Amazon. I greatly appreciate any kind words. Even one or two sentences go a long way. The number of reviews an ebook receives greatly improves how well an ebook does on Amazon.

Amazon – www.amazon.com/author/craigmartelle

BookBub – https://www.bookbub.com/authors/craig-martelle

Facebook – www.facebook.com/authorcraigmartelle

My web page – www.craigmartelle.com

That's it—break's over, back to writing the next book. Peace, fellow humans.

AUTHOR NOTES - MICHAEL ANDERLE

AUGUST 8, 2018

THANK YOU for reading this story, and our author notes in the back!

"Rivka can't live and have a future without you."

So, that sentence above was something I was going to tack on to the first paragraph when it hit me how true it is. We (the bigger 'we' of Indie Authors in general) only have so much time in our lives. Some of us are independently wealthy. (Not me, but I hear there is at least one Indie Author who is independently wealthy. I imagine they have a Unicorn that is twelve inches tall for a pet, or maybe a tiny dragon.)

However, most of us work for our living whether that is work full time in writing and publishing (me) or they work at another job and write part-time (many, many others.)

Either way, our time is limited, and we have to decide where that time is going to go. For some authors, our favorite character was accepted by fans and became a way for us to both feed our families and write about who we want. For others, we have so many characters that we can only choose the characters that resonate with the fans.

Why? Well, in a word, income.

If it takes anywhere from two weeks to three months to write a book, that book needs to be contributing to our income as much as possible. So, characters that resonate and pull in the fans who WANT to read the next book become a very important aspect of choosing what (or who) to write about next.

This isn't always true, of course. Sometimes characters' scream to get out of our heads and for some writers, they MUST get that out of their heads before moving on. Brownstone, for example, was a character that I really, really wanted to write about but the fans wanted more Bethany Anne.

So, I delivered.

Not only to please the fans (thank you so much for pushing me along!) but also because Bethany Anne stories *sold.*

There, I said it. I admitted that income was a driving factor.

Once I completed my twenty-one books for Bethany Anne, I took a three-month sabbatical to get out other stories that I had wanted to see the light of day (Protected by the Damned (Michael Todd) and The Unbelievable Mr. Brownstone.)

Now to explain how that affects Rivka.

Craig has MULTIPLE series he works on. He is a beast when it comes to writing (seriously, I'm not joking. Check out the story he wrote in a weekend one-time at Gary-Con.) But even Craig has to make decisions on which series to move forward, next.

Rivka's story usurped the next Terry Henry Bad Company story in the queue (and I'm happy to admit as a fan, I helped push my own character back a release.) Craig was going to write Bad Company, then Rivka 2... But, after some cajoling, Rivka 2 became the first, with Bad Company becoming the second.

However, Craig didn't want to let down the Bad Company fans, so he made sure there were some scenes with our lovable T.H. in this story.

As an author, we have our favorite characters we wish to write about. Then, we have the characters our fans want us to write about, and somewhere in the middle, we meet.

For any authors you follow and read, 'vote' with your reviews and messages on Facebook or other places to encourage your favorite characters to get their next story. Admittedly, that can be a challenge if five thousand fans want the next book in a series, and you plus one other person want the next one in another of your author's series. (If that happens, I suggest premeditated begging, or offering ways to make it happen. That will have to be the subject of another author note sometime.)

So, for Rivka to continue living and existing, feel free to pester the shit out of Craig to write more of her. I did my job and moved her from #2 in the queue, to #1, and now we have her book right here, right now. *It's your turn to turn up the heat for book 03.*

"Rivka can't live and have a future without you."

Ad Aeternitatem,

Michael Anderle

Craig Martelle's other books (listed by series)

Terry Henry Walton Chronicles (co-written with Michael Anderle) – a post-apocalyptic paranormal adventure

Gateway to the Universe (co-written with Justin Sloan & Michael Anderle) – this book transitions the characters from the Terry Henry Walton Chronicles to The Bad Company

The Bad Company (co-written with Michael Anderle) – a military science fiction space opera

End Times Alaska (also available in audio) – a Permuted Press publication – a post-apocalyptic survivalist adventure

The Free Trader – a Young Adult Science Fiction Action Adventure

Cygnus Space Opera – A Young Adult Space Opera (set in the Free Trader universe)

Darklanding (co-written with Scott Moon) – a Space Western

Judge, Jury, & Executioner – a space opera adventure legal thriller

Rick Banik – Spy & Terrorism Action Adventure

Become a Successful Indie Author – a non-fiction work

Metamorphosis Alpha – stories from the world's first science fiction RPG

The Expanding Universe – science fiction anthologies

Shadow Vanguard – a Tom Dublin series

Uprise Saga – an Amy DuBoff series

Enemy of my Enemy (co-written with Tim Marquitz) – A galactic alien military space opera (coming late summer of 2018)

Superdreadnought (co-written with Tim Marquitz) – a military space opera (coming fall of 2018)